# THE
# WELL
OF
# TRAPPED
# WORDS

Selected Stories

by

Sema Kaygusuz

Translated by

Maureen Freely

# Contents

# Zilşan's Feet

I

THEY KNOW ZILŞAN from her handbag. That's how it is with some girls: people know them from their handbags.

It's red. A holiday gift from the house where they go to clean – if anything so old and out of fashion can be called a gift, that is. The leather is beginning to scale off. The straps are too long for Zilşan, so she has to knot them. And naturally they bite into her shoulder, which now has a groove in it, deep and purple. She has knots all over her. On skirts that are too long, and bras that are one or two sizes too big, and coats with shredded linings. This is a girl whose life is fading at the creases. Its multi-coloured fabric is fast unravelling.

She gets cold. Every season of the year, she gets cold. A pair of normal pants, over which she puts a pair of woollen pants, over which she puts a nylon petticoat, over which she puts a skirt two sizes too big. Everything she owns, she wears – layer over layer. Because her skin can't breathe, it perspires. Her back is always drenched. On her skin she carries the map of an imaginary country. Its sores never heal. Its sores carry the anguish of a city famous for its hills.

On the days she bleeds, her temper is short. She longs, without hope, to be delivered from this staleness, to be light enough to fly with the wind. Even water tastes harsh to her. Any dish containing ground meat revolts her. Everything she touches seems to stick to her skin. But most of all, it's her

1

own blood that shames her. Terrified that a single drop might seep through her skirt, she piles on the layers. And if she jumps at the slightest hint of cool air, it's fear of blood that's worrying her: fear that one drop of blood on her skirt might strip her naked for all to see.

Undressing takes as long as a funeral. When she takes off her stockings, she gets covered in dust. As each garment is cast off, another layer of dust rises into the air. By the time she's undressed, she's drowning in a sea of dust. These are the words that dry the muddy suburbs. She scratches between her never-aired legs. All night long, she scratches until she breaks the skin. Here and there, her pimples get infected. Small aggravations turn into great furies. Only her feet are beautiful. Her toes are small, and lily white, with pearly nails. The rounded bones of her delicate ankles are as smooth as glass; the skin from her heels to her arches blushed with pink. Anyone who only saw her bare feet wouldn't dream they belonged to Zilşan.

There's a skyscraper nearby. A gigantic mall. Reflected in Zilşan's eyes, it shimmers. In this rough-hewn neighbourhood, there could be no image more useless. It's a fearful giant, making the shantytown still clinging to the side of the hill so much smaller, so much uglier. It blocks out the sun, and then the people move on. It's so big that if it collapsed, Zilşan would be caught under the rubble, even this far away. It's so far away that Zilşan would have to run through the mud for half an hour to get there. And when she does, she can't bring herself to go inside. She is sure that if she did, every last object in every last shop window would turn into a monster. She'd freeze in fright.

On the billboards advertising the mall, there's a huge painted hand, sparkling with a single diamond. This is what she stares at all day long, while waiting for Murat. The skyscraper is a giant prism that sparkles with the night's blue lights, a monster that swallows up the young people of the suburbs and holds them inside. It boasts beautiful faces, and beautiful hands, but in stormy weather it roars with each breath. Has Murat thought about Zilşan even once since the mall opened? As he strolls up and down the skyscraper's clean and slippery corridors, day and night, does he ever tire of the sights? Every morning Zilşan steals a cigarette from her father's pocket and stands in front of the skyscraper, waiting for Murat to appear. As the day wears on, she bows under the weight of her heavy clothes. She's so ugly, so very ugly, and as ground down by poverty as a girl can be.

One day she can't bear it anymore and goes straight up to the entrance. The automatic doors slide open. The air rushing out is warm, and sweet as sugar. Startled, Zilşan steps back. The glass panels close. She moves a few steps forward, and they open up again. Then again they close. One step forward – open sesame! One step back – close sesame! A nervous giggle. Then suddenly there's a man standing in front of her. He has rings under his eyes and a detector rod in his hands and he's dressed in navy blue. He says nothing, but he cuts her to shreds with his eyes:

'How do you think you're going to get in when you don't have the faintest idea how to pass through a door (do you really think you do it by waving your arms around like that?), but first, you'll have to give an account of yourself, you'll have to tell us what you're doing here, and, if you have evil intentions, well then let's hear them, and that way we can protect the people who need to be protected from you, we can turn off the lights and hide, or close down the entrances to this place where the walls inside are made of metal and there are bubbles filled with human breath and monsters speaking languages you don't know, or you can come on in and see what goes on in a skyscraper, but show one drop of blood and you're dead, one drop of filth, you hear, but come on in, see couples arm-in-arm, sharing heartbreak, come inside and join the rat race, come and see how the moving staircase cries, each and every time it comes full circle, and see the lift that sobs every time it goes up, because it's afraid of heights, yes, there's a wild carnival going on inside here, a festival the likes of which you've never seen, where there's fair skin for sale, and noble complexions, and acres of good luck charms, and pearls and rubies and perfect geometries, all accounted for, come in and see for yourself but did you think any of them could be eaten like sugarplums and sweets?'

The man in navy blue touches everyone else just once with his detector rod, with a squawk, but he touches Zilşan all over. From her scaling leather bag he removes sheets of gilded paper, a stale stick of neon pink lipstick, a clutch of ballpoint pens, and a compact mirror with a cracked cover – all the accessories, in short, that a girl who is hopeless at playing house might think she'll need. As she goes up the escalator, she looks around in awe. The spotlights make all the things in the windows sparkle and hop. But they drain the colour out of people. She hears noises from the top floor. Chewing, and slurping, and the smell of kebabs. Reluctantly she gulps it in, prey to a hunger that seems to come down to her from her grandfather. She can recognise the shantytown boys at a glance. Square-faced boys with bushy black hair, sitting around aluminium tables with their one glass of Coca-Cola, all eyes on the girls striding past in their shiny high-heeled shoes. With a curiosity that bulges their pleated trousers, into which they've stuffed their shirts, they watch every woman who walks past, young and old, pregnant and lame. As they smoke their cigarettes down to white ash, they dream of being caressed by a fair hand. When they get bored, they kill time by going for long strolls around the mall. The secret cameras track their every move. And when Zilşan catches sight of Murat… well, for every four boys, there's one Murat.

Hiding behind a large palm tree made from fireproof fabric, she watches him. On his flat, smooth countenance she can see no sign of the sweetheart who once made her heart jump with naughty words. A great pit has opened up. She will carry on wandering like a ghost through the mall until closing time, from the first floor to the seventh, from the east wing to the west.

4

Zilşan looks with loathing at her muddy boots. If she can enter the mall, she can enter a shop, too. She watches a salesman serve his customers. He takes a sparkling pair of golden shoes straight out of their box and fits them right away. Her own feet hide like little trinkets under many layers of skirts.

Then, almost unaware of it she too is trying on shoes. But before she dare look at herself in the mirror, the air begins to call to her! Begins to sing! Terror streaks through Zilşan as her feet begin to splay. They get bigger and bigger, growing callouses, growing gnarled. Her toenails curl in. From this day on, she will never again wish for anything new.

She flees the skyscraper. Her sanitary pad slips sideways and sticks to her leg; wet with panic, she hurls herself up the unpaved hills, hopping over the construction rubble. The colours seem to darken, as the shantytown's zinc roofs begin to talk. Inside this noise she hears another noise, and inside that noise something else, very faint – inside a ringing knock, for example, or a knocking ring – like a sad lament, at first, and then a megaphone's wild laughter.

Then crows. So many crows. Crows circling over a deathbed. A long and black procession of infectious diseases – hepatitis, strokes, all the known causes of early death. They have settled on Zilşan's aunt and there they wait. The shantytown is full of people – women wailing in the courtyard, curious children, leaning from windows. The house shakes itself off like a wet dog; the crows all take flight at the same instant. Standing at the aunt's head are two brothers and one son, beating their chests. They've tied rags to her aunt's chin and feet. On her chest, the customary breadknife, to keep her body from swelling. Zilşan lets out a scream, a heart-wrenching wail, soaring higher than the skyscraper. She's still too young to know how to hold back her tears. There was no one like her aunt, her immaculate aunt, always scrubbing the floors with Arab soap, so fragrant. She was the shantytown's shining white hope. Zilşan makes her way through the crowd to rest her head on her aunt's chest. When she lifts up her head, she sees her aunt is about to speak. Her lips are curled, as if she's taken a deep breath to consider what she's about to say. Her hair seems to be growing as fast as her face is changing. But Zilşan can convince no one that her aunt is still alive. For days, she keeps pleading with them not to bury her alive. Since then, her feet have been bleeding, and are covered with sores.

★

30<sup>th</sup> July 1997

*Dear Brother,*

*After you left for your military service, life here became very difficult. Aunt Seher has passed to the next world, may God protect her. She did not suffer too much, thank God. She spent two painless days in bed, and closed her eyes in peace. I have one other piece of bad news. Zilşan has taken leave of her senses. You know how Aunt Seher would look into the distance and begin to mumble from time to time. Well, it's just like that.*

*In fact, she's been doing this for a while, but we didn't pick up on it. We just thought she was imitating Aunt Seher to attract attention. What did we know… And then she was so afraid of water, and wouldn't wash. The smell was unbearable. What can I say? Maybe it was some sort of illness. On the day our Aunt Seher died, Zilşan went missing, and by the time she came back to the house, she'd lost her wits. She came home with bare feet. The soles were covered in blood! We couldn't work out what had happened to her, and anyway, who has time to look after wounds when someone's died? She went to sit at our Aunt's side and cried all night. Our mother said don't touch her. Just let her cry. The girl got it into her head that Aunt Seher was still alive.* Auntie is still alive, *the girl kept moaning. Was it something she saw while she was speaking to her? Perish the thought. But you know how much she loved our Aunt Seher. Her death must have been a terrible shock.*

*Now she wears nothing on her feet. Every night, her sores leak bloody pus. We're afraid of gangrene, of course. Her soles have become a mountain of callouses. If you saw Zilşan right now, you wouldn't even recognise her. Our father has been knocking her about lately. He keeps complaining that we got rid of one madwoman, only to get landed with another. Our poor mother is beside herself.*

*My only hope is that you will complete your military service with honour and come back home. When you do, could you please bring Zilşan a pair of slippers? She might just listen to you... But please don't be upset if she doesn't recognise you.*

*With admiring embraces, I kiss your eyes,*

*Selvi*

# Halfway Down the Middle

ON A SULTRY SEPTEMBER morning, in the hills of Bornova, in the neighbourhood of Tenekeciler, a bad smell of unknown origin came floating through the streets. From the outset, no one believed it came from the rubbish left outside each door, or the sewage surfacing to the west of the city, or the rubber tyres burned by the gypsies in the adjoining neighbourhood. The stink was so strong, and so revolting, that it kept people awake at night; it seemed to stick to their skin like manure, and before they established that it came from a human body, they wasted many days searching elsewhere for its source, washing and rinsing, 40 times over, and beating their cotton bed linen, and raking their gardens, and looking everywhere for dead cats and dogs, and searching each others' faces for signs of shame, and asking each other leading questions. What brought the neighbourhood together was the knowledge that they were all equally affected by the awful stink, which reminded them of burnt meat, rotten fruit, clotting blood, mouldy food, and so much else: no one was spared. Then, when Gülümser Hanımteyze showed her pale face to the world for the first time in a month, a strange new rumour would spread through the streets: Ömer Bey had begun to rot.

None of the neighbours could find the courage to pay more than one visit to the house that Gülümser Hanımteyze shared with Ömer Bey. One by one, and in order of age, they descended on the sick room, hoping to catch Ömer Bey before he drew his last breath, searching for clues that might confirm what they'd heard. Even Naci, the hypochondriac confectioner, went to see him: after taking one short look at Ömer Bey, he ran outside crying, 'Oh, woe is me, Ömer Bey. What's become of you? What a terrible shame! It looks like his stomach has been shot with a cannon! All his insides have come pouring out! He's rotting before our eyes, the poor man! Dear God, why this wound? Why this punishment?'

Ömer Bey would lie on the sofa bed in the sitting room, placid and showing no signs of pain while he swam inside a deeper grief, unaware of his own history, in the manner of a much-visited shrine. Gülümser Hanımteyze would try to keep her husband uncovered, as if she wished to advertise the extent of the tragedy. Perhaps he really was in pain, or perhaps the wound needed airing. No doubt she could never get used to that terrible smell, which was bound to wear her down.

She would not refrain from offering her visitors pomegranate sherbet, even though she knew they would refuse it, or wafting around like a shivering shadow, as though this might distract visitors from the untidy state of the house. Before the visitors so much as asked, she would bring them up to date with his condition, swaying as she fixed her eyes on the middle distance. She would utter the same words in the same tone of voice, always pausing at the same points in the story she had invented for them, never once stumbling over a word, like a criminal with a memorised alibi, before moving on to the bit where she would cry:

'Dearest neighbour, it started a month ago. I woke up one morning, and – forgive me for speaking frankly about domestic matters – there was nothing in the house for breakfast. No oil, no olives… My blood pressure had risen the day before, so I'd not gone out to the market. Fearing that this man here might get angry, I got the tea going as quickly as I could. Best if I make menemen[1], I thought. So I chopped up some parsley, and an onion – and what cheese we had left. I cooked it up well, so he wouldn't grumble. I brought it out

---

1. A traditional Turkish breakfast dish, similar to shakshouka.

to the table, and divided it down the middle. He ate one half and I ate the other. Ömer Efendi had not even finished his half when he went into convulsions! First I thought he had an upset stomach. The eggs were ten days old, after all, so maybe they'd gone off, and made him sick. But I ate it too, and nothing happened to me. He was rolling on the floor, saying someone was stabbing him in the stomach, and I had no idea what to do. Towards evening, he flopped and went still. The little man slept all night, like a log. But when he woke up the next day, he started scratching his stomach. I ate the same thing as he did, but I certainly wasn't scratching like that. Don't scratch, I said. You'll hurt yourself. He wouldn't listen, he kept scratching, and soon there were little welts all over his skin, and all that scratching made them raw, and soon they started stinking. The bigger the wound, the more it stank. And didn't I treat them with gentian oil? Didn't I scrub them with garlic vinegar? It hardly seemed like a wound anymore, it seemed like some sort of monster. It's eating up his insides. One morning I woke up, and all his skin was gone. Everything that should have been inside was now outside, for all to see. And what a smell. What a smell! Stronger than the earth's embrace. And now I can't get a morsel of food to pass his lips. As for water, I give it to him drop-by-drop. He no longer knows who he is. All day long he sleeps and wheezes. He hears no sounds. Never opens his eyes. The man is dying before our eyes.'

The residents of the Tenekeciler District, who generally died from heart attacks or insidious cancers or asthma attacks that were the bequests of their ancestors, learned something new from Ömer Bey's wound: that we each have to face our own death is a consolation to be accepted with grace. Whatever else it is, death takes its only inspiration from life. The pains and cuts and ruptures it brings us come from the same source as life itself. Someone else's hand, someone else's influence. And who can say what happened to Ömer Bey, before that sore ate up his skin? Maybe a chirping cricket disturbed his sleep in August, when he slept so poorly anyway.

Maybe the full moon took refuge in the belly of the spiteful night, to escape from the black hands of the clouds passing before its face; maybe it chose to hide in a house in Tenekeciler, the self-same house that Gülümser Hanımteyze shared with Ömer Bey. And then, who knows, maybe the mice on the veranda climbed up into the arbour, to munch noisily on the unripe grapes. At this point, an ill-tempered owl might have arrived, to take over the night watch with its gentle breathing. As light filtered into the sky, the sounds of the day might have combined to make a gentle moan, seeping through the cracks in the windows and the doors, to pass over Gülümser Hanımteyze's eyelids. And suddenly, the woman might have woken up, and even if she had heard none of this, even if she had never looked up into the sky, or noticed the owl, and the mice in her grape vines, it still could have happened. Who knows?

And so it was that the Tenekeciler District, so long accustomed to quiet, murmuring deaths, was confronted by one of impudence and ostentation – a death that was, with its bad smells, reminiscent of the ghost stories they had abandoned so very long ago. For the first time, they would prepare to mourn together. This time, the happy news they so urgently awaited would be Ömer Bey's death. A great death indeed. In time, it would spread like ivy to the end of every cul-de-sac, and turn to stone. The huge wound – wavering somewhere between saffron yellow and charcoal – would carry on expanding, to cover the body, one millimetre at a time. The skin on his chest would dry up and turn red. The exposed ribs would shrink, like pieces of chalk. The dark lilac blotches on the legs would grow until the legs were all purple, and as cold as ice. Gülümser Hanımteyze would sleep fitfully as she awaited the angel of death, who might arrive at any minute, and as she prepared herself for his gentle blue voice, she would hear even the walls creaking. And when a child three streets away fell off his bike, she would know him from his cry alone. So what a pity it was that the angel of death did not bring this anguished vigil to an end with his

12

luminous sentence, and his string of rounded words, which did not travel from left to right, but right to left. With this wound, she would retreat into questions about whys and wherefores; she would tire of her prayers; they would come to feel like olive pits too long in the mouth.

A few weeks later, Ömer Bey's moans would stop at last, and there would follow another silent funeral in Bornova's Tenekiciler District. Thus he would be delivered both from the stink and from the gruesome death that would continue to haunt them. Most people saw no need to go to Gülümser Hanımteyze to offer their condolences, because there was nothing new left to know. The only mystery remaining was Gülümser Hanımteyze's sleepless night.

★

Let's return now to the beginning of August. This summer had been milder than the ones that came before. The first house in Tenekeciler to turn off its lights that night was Gülümser Hanımteyze's. Towards morning, the air rang with a cricket's song. Gülümser Hanımteyze heard nothing. The full moon, sitting in the loveliest patch of sky, was waving its slender fingers, painting the sky with shafts of rosy light. What a shame that she didn't see the sky. As the mice on the veranda climbed up into the arbour to munch on unripe grapes, an owl hooted, somewhere near the house. But Gülümser did not hear it. As the sun's feeble light drew a red line across the dawn, she looked up at the ceiling and took a deep breath. Ömer Bey was taking over the room with his wheezing and snoring, and pushing his wife into a corner. Too quietly for anyone to hear, Gülümser Hanımteyze mumbled these doomed words: 'There is nothing left for breakfast.'

# Many Years Ago, I was Standing in a Meydan

IT MUST HAVE BEEN about a year ago. We were in Hüseyin Abi's barber shop. You know the day Kekil Dede[2] untied his tongue? Well, it was that day. Hüseyin was shaving the back of Kekil Dede's neck, it was almost as if he could tap into any thought floating through the head beneath his fingers.

Just to keep the banter going, he said, 'Kekil Dede, you have nothing in the world, and you're all alone. Why don't we marry you off to Gevher, the widow of our dear departed Hüseyin? You could travel through the rest of life together.'

I was watching the two men in the mirror – Hüseyin, with Kekil Dede perched in a chair in front of him. When Hüseyin the barber had said his piece, Kekil lifted his head as if to address his answer to me, but then, as I might not be in a position to understand the nature of the affront, he took a deep breath, and, how can I put it, he spat out two words.

'No!' he said. And again. 'No!'

And then, in the most resentful voice you could imagine, he began to say the strangest thing (even as I relate this, I realise I'm unable to convey the thing I'd like to describe above all, which is that moment just before someone lets a sentence loose, that split second when all you have is the foul smell). But as I was saying, Kekil Dede lifted his head slightly, looked me straight in the eye and began to speak:

---

2. Dede is the Turkish word for 'grandfather', though not always reffering literally to a biological grandfather.

'Many years ago, I was standing in a meydan[3]. I was just twelve years old. We were surrounded by soldiers. They had gathered everyone in the villages of Qawume and Textêxel who came from the Demenan tribe. There was a woman amongst them. She had wrapped her infant around her neck like a double chin. Had she had enough strength, she would have swallowed the baby whole and hid it inside her. Her scarf was slipping off her head, her golden locks were slipping down her face.

'The village muhtar[4] surrendered everyone to the soldiers – men, women and children. Then there was a roar and a crash, and the girls got mixed up with the boys, the babies with the old men. When that woman died, there were no other women left. All the women in the world were dead. And now you're proposing a woman to a man who was widowed at the age of twelve.'

Neither Hüseyin Abi nor I knew how we felt about what we'd just heard. It was just a lot of strange names from distant lands. If a few scenes did play before our eyes, they were like things in a film. What I mean to say is – we were shocked. Our ears were ringing with shock. We were not moved by what Kekil Dede had told us. Now you are probably going to tell me I am callous… But it wasn't callousness that kept me from understanding Kekil Dede; it was ignorance. Also, in the coffeehouses in these parts, they're always telling hunting stories. And they're so very distressing, you know, I can't bear hearing them but I still listen. To make their stories more painful still, and also more exciting, they make the boars sound like swashbucklers, and the deer like young women. And may God forgive us, but we just sit there gaping. It was the same when we were listening to Kekil Dede.

As for Hüseyin the barber, don't even ask. He was even more bewildered than I was. He kept shaving the same spot. He was in danger of cutting the man's neck. He just stood

---

3. A public space.
4. The elected head of a village.

16

there in shock. What soldiers? What villages? What is this man raving about? He just couldn't figure it out. He didn't know if he should ask a question or just stay silent. He looked over at us – we weren't saying a word either. Kekil Dede rose from his chair, put on his jacket, and left the shop. It was a very long time before we saw him again.

We only knew him as Kekil, actually. We were the ones who added the Dede. We knew nothing about where he came from, or who he was. But I've known him for 20 years now. I can still remember his first day in Havsa. The moment he stepped into our terminal here in Havsa he came straight into the drivers' coffeehouse. In those days I was driving a dolmuş[5] between Cumhuriyet Mahalle and the city centre. I noticed the old man at once. He was carrying a little suitcase, and he was wearing one of those overcoats with deep cuffs, the type that retired civil servants like to wear. I saw at once that he was not from our parts.

I sat down next to him, and I asked him, 'Who are your people? Who have you come to see?' He had nothing to tell me. He just asked if I knew of a cheap hotel.

'How long are you staying?' I asked.

'A long time,' he said.

I had a modest little house I'd inherited from my aunt – pretty much a ruin.

'Forget hotels,' I said, 'let's find you a house, it will end up being cheaper.' And so I pulled a few things together, two blankets and a quilt, a little gas cylinder, whatever we had in the house that the wife didn't need any more, and I moved Kekil into my aunt's house. He was probably around sixty years old at the time. But if you looked at his legs and his feet, and his swollen eyes, which looked like they'd taken a few punches, he looked more like a man in his eighties. On the day he moved in, Kekil paid a year's rent up front. When the wife saw all that money, she ran straight over to him.

'Let me clean this place up,' she said. 'Let me wash the windows, we can't have you living in a place this dirty and dusty.'

---

5. A shared taxi that runs a set route between towns or city districts.

But what a contrary man this Kekil was.

'What's this dirt to you?' That's what he said to my Esma. 'Never come here again,' he said, and he threw her out of the house. That's when we realised that we were going to have to keep our distance from this strange man until he came round. But that never happened.

The summer passed, and then the winter. Kekil had still not come out of himself. So now I was getting a little concerned. We had given him a house, no questions asked, and what was he up to in there – making bootleg rakı? Dealing hashish? Selling weapons? The last thing we wanted was trouble. One Sunday I picked up a few of the gözlemes[6] Esma likes to make, the ones with all the herbs, and went over to Kekil's house. And what do I find when I step inside but every cat in the neighbourhood that was missing an ear or a tail, every blind, lame, mangy dog he could find; he'd brought them all into the house. It stank to high heaven and when they smelled the gözlemes, the cats started jumping as high as my shoulders. There was nothing left you could call furniture. Everything from the curtains to the sofa covers were in tatters. Newspapers on the floor, macaroni strewn all over the place, battered water containers. If Esma ever saw this, she'd flip. I started breathing through my mouth, to protect myself from the stink. When Kekil shooed the cats away, they scattered everywhere; then he fed them all bits of gözleme.

From that day on, I never set foot in the house. If anyone asked me who Kekil was and what he was up to, I just said he was cracked and left it at that. To tell the truth, by then I'd realised what a miserable person Kekil was – he even, how shall I say it, seemed to have a *need* for misery. He wanted to be surrounded by crying, moaning animals. So as not to disturb the man, I kept well away.

Months later, Kekil at last began to come down to the market. He's human, after all, and sooner or later he was bound to get bored. He waited and waited, but the dogs

---

6. A savoury, stuffed flatbread.

never learned to talk, of course. Grim as ever, he would come into the coffeehouse, greeting no one. If I said hello to him, all I would get was the same word back. Then we began to notice that it wasn't just people that Kekil stayed away from, but also the state. When there was a census, he wouldn't open the door for the census-taker, for example. He never visited the muhtar's office, never voted, never went to the post office, or the governor's office, or the council, or the bank. Every once in a while he'd go off to Edirne, and come back with cash. There were all sorts of rumours about him. Some people said he owned a chain of leather shops in Istanbul; others said that he had Byzantine treasures he'd found in Kütahya, and was now selling them on the black market to Greeks. No one dared say a thing to Kekil Dede's face. Not once was he seen at a funeral, a wedding, a circumcision, or at Friday prayers. The only places he went were the coffeehouse and the meyhane[7]. He would sit in silence amongst the drunks, the card players and the men watching television, and if anyone spoke to him, he'd just say, 'I must be on my way.' The only ones he'd talk to were me and Hüseyin the barber. Nothing he told us made much sense. He said one thing and then the opposite, if you know what I mean.

So it was after rambling on for exactly 20 years that this Kekil Dede finally said something that actually meant something. But he spoke as if he were speaking to the air, and Hüseyin Abi and I were still scratching our heads when he upped and left.

I kept thinking about what he'd said. And then a few weeks later, what do I see but Kekil Dede hobbling down to the market. His right leg seemed shorter than his left leg (but it would be hard for me to describe his particular way of hobbling; it seemed habitual, or even part of his personality). I went over to him, and said, 'Come on now, let's get you to a doctor.'

---

7. A traditional tavern.

He looked as if he were about to curse me. 'Are you blind, son?' he said, 'I've always been crippled.'

'What are you saying? My dear Dede, you were never crippled like this until today. If you'd been crippled, wouldn't we have called you Kekil the Cripple?'

Tears came to his eyes then, and I swear that his chin was quivering when he spoke: 'There was a mill. They took us to the cliffs behind the mill and lined us up in three rows, one behind the other. I was in the third row, at the back. My great uncle Mustafa was in the front line. The soldiers aimed their rifles at us. I wasn't thinking about death right then, because death is God's will. But I was thirsty, and the bubbling brook just behind me was making me thirstier. I said to myself, well, when I'm dead I won't be thirsty anymore, or hungry. The soldiers were now standing shoulder to shoulder. There was a lieutenant with tiny eyes, and he was looking at his soldiers, not at us. Walking back and forth, he said, "When you fire, don't you all aim at the same point." Then my uncle Mustafa who was in the front row spoke to those around him. "They'll shoot us first, so when we're hit, let's fall back, so that we can save those lying beneath us. Just remember that we shall be travelling down the road to Kerbela[8] as martyrs." I'll never forget there was a soldier on the right flank who caught the word Kerbela in my uncle's Kurdish words and began to cry. Hanging from his shoulder was a rifle with a bayonet, but there he was, leaning his head against the handle, crying. Then they raked us with bullets. Oh how those bullets flew. One went through my hand. Such heat I felt then. Mustafa fell on his godson, and his godson fell on me. I was left lying underneath my tribe. The shooting stopped. There was moaning here and there, but I kept quiet. The lieutenant ordered his soldiers to leave no one alive. He had a shrill voice, this infidel. The soldiers came towards us with bayonets, to kill us all off for good. A bayonet hurts more than a bullet. I wouldn't wish it on my worst enemy. Not even the bravest

8. The holy Iraqi city of pilgrimage.

20

youth could bear that without screaming. The whole earth was screaming by then, and the sky with it. After they had bayoneted all the dead and wounded, they threw them over the cliff, towards Munzur. One by one, the bodies above me were being raised up. Then I looked, and there he was – the crying soldier! He could tell that I was only playing dead. He glanced over at the lieutenant, and then at the other soldiers. He stabbed my thigh with the bayonet and rolled me down. And I've been limping ever since.'

I'm not going to lie. Right then, I didn't believe what I'd just heard. My mind wasn't taking it in, but other parts of me were. My eyes believed. My nose believed. The cigarette I'd lit while listening, and the embers, they believed him, too. But I refused. I didn't sleep a wink that night. Hüseyin the barber was the only one I told Kekil's story to. He didn't believe it either. But why would he? Kekil Dede was for us someone who had come from the other end of the Earth. Whatever he said, he was still a stranger; whatever stories he told. And anyway, that life he led with all those mangy animals, it wasn't a life, and somehow we had not found a proper place for this man in our district of Havsa. We knew there was a river called the Munzur in Tunceli province, on account of that dam they were building, but we had no idea what happened there when Kekil was 12 years old.

Some time later, I saw Kekil Dede at the bus terminal. Probably he was just back from one of his trips to Edirne. There was a dirty bandage around his right hand. 'What happened to your hand, Kekil Dede?'

First he swore blind. 'You have no more brains than a loaf of bread! My hand is in pieces, it's a useless wreck, haven't you ever noticed?' He had a hard time staying upright while he was talking. His face was a mess, and so was his hair, and his eyes were bloodshot.

I said what I had to say: 'Please don't take offence, Dede. You're right, of course, that bullet went through your hand.' That softened him a bit; off he went, mumbling to himself.

Then, in the middle of the terminal, he stopped in his tracks. The people getting off buses, and pulling their suitcases, they all passed around Kekil, as if he were a tree, but none of them touched him.

The porters were making a racket, and Cemal the snack-bar man had turned up his television full volume to watch a horse race, and buses were manoeuvring – turning and parking. This was the commotion that Kekil Dede was standing there watching, as if it were only a matter of time before he vanished inside it. Then suddenly he turned around and hobbled back to me.

'It was the dogs that upset me the most. It's dogs that make my heart ache. Did you know that?'

'Dogs?' I said.

'Yes, dogs,' he said. 'When the dogs got hungry, they started eating the bodies. It took them ten days to get used to human meat. And once they'd eaten human flesh, they became human. Their expressions changed. Their voices, too. Then the dead no longer satisfied them. They began to eat the living. They began to set traps in the forests, the little devils. They'd hide in caves and lie in wait.'

I took Kekil by the arm, to walk together, very slowly. Whenever he spoke, he slowed down even more. 'There was this soldier… the crying soldier. He threw me down to the Munzur, and I grabbed a tree that'd taken root amidst the rocks, and for four days and four nights, I hid on a ledge beneath it. The water had worked its way inside my head, and I was mad with pain. The water was so close, but not a drop flowed down my throat. The Munzur was red with blood, my uncles were swimming inside it – how could I drink it? So I clawed and I clawed until at last I made myself a hollow. And there I stayed for 25 days, half-conscious, without a crust of bread. Those willows I could see, those poplars, they were all strangers to me. I didn't even consider the blacksnakes or the centipedes or the ants. My skin crawled with the insects that fed on the corpses. I can still feel the sting of those ants. With their pincer jaws, they were eating me alive. Many days later,

I felt something heavy on me. A big dog was sniffing at my wound, nuzzling my flesh with his nose. And I came to life. Anger swept through me. You know how animals will go after an enemy, well I did the same. I was going to vanquish him, I swear! The animal was snarling, and I was roaring. Then suddenly the dog gave a heart-rending yelp, and I looked up and there was the soldier who'd bayoneted me, plunging the bayonet into the dog. And that was when I saw my fate written in that soldier's eyes. He was looking at a body that had been half chewed by ants, a body that centipedes had made their home and that dogs saw as a corpse. I looked at him standing there with the bayonet in his hand. Was he Azrael,[9] or was he Cebrael?[10] I couldn't say.

'"I'm hungry," I said, in Turkish. I was so hungry that I could have said it in any language under the sun. The soldier reached into his shirt and brought out a piece of dry bread. Before he handed it over, he asked me whether or not I had a coin. That's how I knew he was a man made of flesh and blood. He was not as wild as a dog, nor as slow as a centipede. He was just another man, like us. I handed over the coins I had hidden in my belt. And he handed me the bread. I can no longer remember if I took it or not, ate it or not. When I reached out for the bread, I blacked out, I fainted.'

Those were the last words I would ever hear from Kekil Dede. As he spoke, he began to fade away. Slipping out of my arm, he pushed me back slightly. He staggered off under his own steam, and as he walked, all the wounds from his childhood opened up again. And I cannot begin to describe the pain in my heart as I watched his slow retreat.

A few days later, we were woken by barking dogs. They were Kekil's dogs, and they were standing at the top of the Cumhuriyet Mahalle, howling. I knew at once that Kekil had died. In the morning, when I went over to his house, I found all the cats of the neighbourhood with missing legs or tails

---

9. The Angel of Death.
10. The Angel of Revelation.

lying over his body, like a blanket. All I could see of the man was his head. His eyelashes were crusted and his mouth was half-open. Only God knows why, but at that moment Kekil's face looked so very different from the one I knew. By dying, the little man had become someone else altogether. And maybe, when a man's face relaxes, all its memories are erased, because there was nothing left there of the Kekil I had known.

When they came from the council to do the death certificate, there was a big commotion.

'This one's been dead a long time. What's his name?'

'Kekil.'

'And his surname?'

'We don't know…'

'Impossible,' said the official. 'Go and find his identity card.' The gravediggers rolled Kekil into a sheet and took him to the council. And Esma and I covered our mouths with muslin and went into the house to hunt down his identity card. We went through his chest of drawers, we checked under the bed, and inside the wardrobes, turned the whole place upside down. And then I remembered. Twenty years earlier, Kekil Dede had been carrying a small suitcase. It must be in there, I thought. And at the very back of the cabinet in the storeroom, under the piles of newspaper, we found the suitcase.

A pile of papers, letters in old Turkish, and envelopes… The identity card was in the lining, in a folder together with the deeds to three houses in Adana. The photograph on his identity card was very old. It showed a solidly built man in his forties. On his face he bore no signs of having once been wounded by a bayonet, or left crippled, or chewed by dogs, or any of the other miseries he had told me about. His name was Nusret Karaman. He was born in Adana. There was nothing about Kekil, in other words. The earth had opened up and swallowed him. It was as if there had never been a man named Kekil.

Later, in a morocco leather folder we found dozens of photographs. This Nusret Bey had even had a wife. They'd sat on a bench together, with their babies on their laps, a waterfall in the background. In another photograph, there were football players, posing in two rows. And goodness me, there he was… Nusret Karaman, which meant that he had played for the 19th May Sports Club. He was standing in the middle, his chest all puffed up. A few other family photos; his sons growing up…grandchildren in his arms… sitting at tables laden with food, drinking rakı… The last photograph we retrieved from the morocco leather case was folded in two. The crease was beginning to tear. A group of smiling soldiers standing, shoulder to shoulder. Their bayonets sunk into the ground. Nusret Karaman is leaning towards an army friend, his misty eyes facing forward. He has yet to come eye-to-eye with a 12-year-old boy in a meydan. He still knows nothing of Kekil. On the back of the photo, in fine handwriting: *Dersim 1938: We vanquished every last Kurd.*

# Cold

THERE'S THIS STRANGE ache in my shoulders. Sometimes I feel like I'm a tortoise. Life seems to me like this shell that was set on my back when I wasn't looking. The longer I drag it, the heavier it gets. The older I get, the greater the burden.

I sit by the window and watch the girl in the apartment across the way; hour after hour, month after month.

Even though she knows I'm watching her, she's never bothered to draw her curtains. In the face of my wish not to be seen, my facelessness – my oppressiveness, even – she is recklessly indifferent. As I watch her from the sitting room, I can never figure out what she is thinking. On her balcony are a few flowerpots, the earth in them is covered with dead leaves. I don't even want to think about why she hasn't cleared them away. Spent lives have their own ways of waiting to be revived, after all; we are not looking at something new here.

She always sits in darkness.

I can see her face in the blue light of the television. She's wearing a sea-green towel dress. It reminds me of the beach dress my mother sewed for me when I was a child. Oh, how I loved that dress, I even wanted to wear it on feast days. My mother and I would argue about it for hours. The colour really suits her, too.

She stretches out on the double sofa.

I look at her eyes and I see no images reflected from the television. She leaves her possessions untouched. It's like she's

27

just putting up with them. The same way she puts up with me.

There once was a strapping young man who paid her frequent visits, always in a white shirt. The sort of young man who reminds you of your age. He had his own key. He'd wander around the girl's sitting room with his mind on other things, taking up all the space. Then he'd string together a few words. It was fun, watching him come and go, but the girl never paid him the slightest attention and I found that interesting. It made no difference to her if White Shirt came or stayed away. She watched him as blankly as she watched television. Well, maybe she laughed about once every 40 years, but I think that was because she had to. The sort of laugh that made me think of yellow taxis, dimly-lit government offices, and my bamboo chair.

So White Shirt would say a few words, and then he'd start kissing her. It didn't surprise me that no one thought to draw the curtains, not in this day and age, but still it bothered me. I'd always choose that moment to go into the kitchen to make myself some rosehip tea. Just once, I watched the whole thing. It tested my nerves watching them make love, and it was so very odd. It was as if she were sleeping with her enemy – as if she had made some sort of pact with this enemy that she had to honour.

A reluctant sort of seduction, in other words. I sometimes wonder how the couples in my circle make love, especially the ones who don't suit each other. Of course, there's no way to find out. But that day, I just couldn't take my eyes off that window across the way. And while I watched them, I could feel all my regrets steaming inside me, and somehow, strangely, washing me clean. You know how if you pour out your troubles, they somehow get worse, or how, if you talk about things that matter very little, they get larger and larger, until there's something sitting in your chest, the size of an egg… While I watched them, I remembered that I too had flesh, fed by blood. I began to cherish my own troubles, I mean to say. I had learned these words by heart: I was the sole owner of all the tumours that would one day consume me. Life would go on, with or without them. Sometimes it happens that those suffering pain come to an agreement with the 'tyrant'. If only to forget the pain for a short while.

Last week there was a great storm, a great downpour, and I felt myself cleansed by the scent of rain wafting through my window. That night, I chose the rain over the girl. But once I'd caught a glimpse of her curled up in a corner, crying. I couldn't take my eyes off her. I was tempted to go over and console her. She looked as helpless as a kitten who'd lost her mother. She put on a pullover, then a cardigan, then a robe, and thick socks. She was chilled to the bone.

But each morning she turns into someone altogether different. I've never seen her wear the same dress twice. Everything about her is always changing – the way she does her hair, the lipstick she puts on, the coloured stockings, the different buckles she puts on her shoes, her skirts. Coming as they do after such melancholy evenings, these morning demonstrations of hope make no sense to me. For a while, I thought I was going to lose my mind. Why, if she can look like someone new each morning, does she crack into pieces the same way each night? She's no different to those flowers in her flowerpots, getting paler every hour. Does she have trouble with her relatives, even as she struggles to honour her obligations? Or is she the sort of intolerable person who makes trouble for everyone crossing her path? Does she concoct sentences full of flattering lies, to wipe away the guilt, trying to talk herself into a friendship that will never blossom? Or is it an impossible love that drives her? Are there times, especially at night, when, having asked herself a few clean questions, she's struck down by the absolute absence of answers? Is she incapable of using those simple words that keep a person upstanding – that enchanting yes, that noble no? Is that why she fades as evening falls? Is she carrying a short winter's day on her back, a petrified fragment of the past, passed down to her from her mother, her grandmother, and her great grandmother? Or is she carrying inside her a fear that was already old when she was born? The fear of being a woman.

One day, when I was waiting for a dolmuş, she said good morning to me from the back of the queue. I heard a tone in her warm and childish voice that was entirely her own. She was treating me the same way she treated White Shirt. As if to say, 'What else can I do? You're here.' That evening, she put her phone book on her lap and rang all the numbers, one by one. But it was impossible to tell from her face whom she mistrusted, or whom she disliked, or whom she'd broken off from, or didn't love, or didn't want to love, or had grown to accept. The 27th person she called was an old lover, I think. He was telling her sweet things, while she fiddled with her hair and stretched herself out on the double sofa, like an elastic band. Most certainly she was saying that she'd been thinking of him for a few days and had decided only that night to call him. And Number 27 seemed to believe her, because the conversation went on for a long time. I tried to imagine how happy this man felt as he put down the phone, never knowing that he was 27th in line to the throne. Yes, certainly, he'd got entirely the wrong idea. When the girl put down the phone, it was only to gaze blankly up at the ceiling, and this struck me as profoundly moving: the sight of someone mentally paralysed by a game, sinking into nothingness.

While I was watching her tonight, I came to understand that she did not love her sea-green dress as much as she used to. She went into the kitchen, to make herself a coffee, I think. Then she sat down right in front of the window, and as she took her first sip, she looked straight at me. For a moment, we were eye to eye. She didn't even give me time to pull back. I took this to mean that she'd decided to look at me before she'd even sat down. Why am I always the one who is late to the party? She had only a few seconds' advantage over me. How can it be that I am now in her thrall? And this after so many long months of just letting me sit here, in my bamboo chair, and never once coming eye to eye! I break away from her stare and go back to watching some children get scolded for dropping a marmalade jar. Cold sweat runs down my back. Now she's going to say something to me, and though I won't be able to hear her, I'll know at once what she's saying. Isn't this how I've always listened to the world? As a delayed response, but also as a game of intuition.

So there we are, nose to nose, close enough to count each other's eyelashes. There's a strange smile on her lips that I find troubling. I begin to feel my hair roots burning, right down to my neck. She's come very close to me. She's ready for me, entirely ready. This much I know: in unexpected encounters, admitting nothing is never enough.

She beckons me to come closer to the window.

What's she going to say? *You've been watching me for months now; aren't you bored yet?* – is that what she's going to say? I've been caught unawares. I'm frightened of her and her television set, and her double sofa, and her sea-green nightgown, and of that wardrobe of hers with all those outfits in it. I feel the disquiet in my mind like a great insurmountable wall, casting a shadow over me. If I am ever to be free of this shadow, I must either claw my way over the wall or walk the full length alongside it. But I'm too old to climb over. Or take my eyes off that woman! My eyebrows, my fingertips, my veins, they're not working. They've walked this wall with me before. So then let's change this wall's position, just as easy as moving my bamboo chair away from the window.

I can't say how long it's taken me to leave my house and reach her door. I might have lingered in my garden, to inspect the ivy. I might have contemplated this tortoise life I complain about. Or I might at least have turned to look up at the window I've left behind, and wonder how many sips of rosehip tea I have left. But I'm in no shape to count.

Her door is ajar.

I'm still not sure I'm expected. She doesn't even come to greet me. It's pitch dark inside. Slowly I take off my shoes and put them where they belong. The flickering light of the television is playing games with the shadows in the room. I feel like I'm walking down an endless hospital corridor. If only I could find a place to hide, a place to take shelter! I don't even know what I'm going to say if we suddenly come face to face.

I find her asleep on the double sofa, hands clasped over her stomach. She has to bend her knees to fit. My guess is she fell asleep out of boredom, fed up from months of waiting for me to pull myself up from my chair and come over. But how can I really know any of this?

How beautiful her hair looks, spread out over that pillow with its lovely floral print. How lovely her quiet chest, and her lightly-curled lips. She's taken the night inside her; she's sleeping the night. I'm so glad she's asleep. How lucky that we don't have to speak. I've been worried she'd pick me apart. But now a velvety sound comes flying in from the past: who was it who said that even my faults became me? Was it my mother?

How lovely this room is. These chairs, this table, the pictures on the wall. I quietly cross the room and turn off the television. The buzz of the darkening screen annoys me. But now it is too dark. Voices, smells, designs, figures, shadows, colours, they're all flowing past. Slowly I begin to tread air. Every dream I have from now on will be filled with anxiety about the future. It's all over. And the wall – I am free of its shadow. Free from this girl who stole my beach dress, from the man who was 27th on the list, from the chair that has brought me such troubles. I lie down next to the woman on the double sofa.

White Shirt stalks around the room, shouting frantically. He holds me tight and cries. He does things he's never done before: caresses my face, kisses my eyes. He begs me to forgive him. He mumbles. It's hard to hear what he's saying. I look without anger at his blurry face. In fact, I never was angry with him. If only I could have warmed to the world enough to be angry.

It makes me feel safe, this fear on White Shirt's face. I can't understand a thing he's saying now. He stares at my white wrists as they turn to red, leaking my scent. My very essence. He stares and screams. He's afraid of losing me. I surrender to the dark with a heavy heart. I am fear, made flesh. I am *his* fear. His fear of failing as a man. He's afraid of colours, of the colours inside us, of the things we dare not open to the world. For the first time, I feel cold without longing for warmth. Oh, how lovely it is to feel cold.

# Yülerzik[11]

IF YOU WANT TO find a yülerzik, the first place you should look is in the shade of the walnut trees. We'll give you a couple of clues, so you can recognise it right away. Maybe there are more than two – maybe, when you see it, you'll find out other things we know nothing about. If you're expecting a plant of extraordinary beauty, you're on the wrong track. Most people make that mistake when they hear the name. Some names dress themselves up in the sounds that come from inside them. But though it might call to mind an embroidered bracelet, a gloomy face, or leaves sharing a branch, the yülerzik is an utterly ordinary plant.

Before you set out, before you find it, you must purify yourself. You must expect nothing from the yülerzik, and remember that it is just standing there, expecting nothing from you. Bear in mind that the day will come when you shall have to sit there like a plant yourself, if only to see life's possibilities more clearly. And that's one of the secrets: the way to approach this plant. This distance between staying and going. You're ready to leave, but the yülerzik is still sitting there; forget at your peril that it does not wait for you.

The moment you see it, you'll change. A new image will take root in your mind. A new kind of green. Its very existence will be proof of an absence. But whether you exist or not, it will go on changing. When the time comes, it will

---

11. A plant used in folk medicine and spiritual practices, the seeds from which are also used to make a red dye.

grow greener if surrounded by greenery. If it is surrounded by plants of a yellow hue, it too will tend to yellow. You know how a plant's fronds, or its roots, its leaves or its smell, are often associated with women? You are going to leave all such lore to one side. What we can see in the yülerzik is something closer to a boy. A loner, jealous and contrary, lean and tensed for battle. A certain, unexpected woodiness. It keeps itself to itself, so that its leaves don't touch other plants, while its stalk grows high. As much as the season permits; as high as its strength allows. This plant is not much of a talker, when it comes down to it. So don't expect any showy red or purple flowers. In spite of its huge leaves and hard thin branches, all you get is – you know the flowers you see on green pepper plants? Well it has bright white flowers just like those. Little, heavy-headed flowers with light-green globes at the centre. When the white petals on the corolla dry up and fall away, these globes begin to grow. When the sun begins to spoil, they turn red. This part is very important, because if you see them at this stage, you can confuse them with a cumin plant. You'll already know about the caraway plant, of course.

You must act as if you have never seen a yülerzik before. You must look with your eyes, and only your eyes. In the natural world, you must never confuse one presence with another. If you mix a yülerzik with a cumin plant, you will, in the first instance, cause the cumin plant injury. If you wish to catch a whiff of its pungent and delicious fragrance, you must watch your step. If you are to embrace the disquiet and heartache of doubt, you must leave behind faith's watertight platitudes and heavy lethargy.

The best thing you can do when you've found your plant is to sacrifice one of its peach-coloured globes. That way you will neither betray the cumin plant nor pledge yourself to the yülerzik. The moment you touch the plant, one of its globes will drop right into the palm of your hand. You'll crush it, and if little black seeds come spilling out, you'll know it's a yülerzik. From then on, you'll recognise these seeds at one glance.

When you find a yülerzik, the way you feel at that moment will determine how you see it. So if there's the smallest curl of a doubt floating through your head, what you'll notice first will be the leaf's latticed texture. You'll regret never having looked at a plant this closely before. You'll tear off a leaf and chew it, taste its green pain without fear. And maybe, at that moment, as you come to see how small and simple this plant is, you'll feel disappointed, and so very lonely, too. And what a terrible feeling that is: with the contortions in your heart, and your secret pain, you will feel yourself a savage, surrounded by strangers with whom you share no tongue. But what a shame it is that the moment you touch a yülerzik, you lose hope, asking yourself what difference there is between this and parsley. In a situation like this, you might need someone to re-acquaint you with the plant. That is when you must remember how long the yülerzik has sat there on its own, and how far you travelled to find it. You can hear all the sounds around you – the birds calling, the weeds crackling, the wind blowing in from afar; you can breathe in the heavy scent of the walnut tree. To rid yourself at once of this noisy crowd, you must see nothing beyond the yülerzik. Do not forget that one day you might stumble over the very thing you knew all along.

And now we have come to a sharp parting of ways. Do you believe in luck? If so, you'll do as so many others have done before you. You'll pluck the plant's little globes and string them up nicely and tie rags between them and hang them up in a part of the house that gets a lot of sun, as a good luck charm. Do that, and the yülerzik will turn its shaved head to gaze at you in misery. If you ask us what we think you should do, we'll say only this, just this one little thing we'd like you to remember: life bequeaths you only those things that go through the mind, and that is why you are never to turn the yülerzik into the sort of empty object that soon slips out of mind. If a good luck charm is all you're after, that's your business, but when you turn a yülerzik into a charm, you are ruining it. Shaming it.

When you find your yülerzik, it might take you aback, with its green shoots, and its wise wooden body. You might feel overcome. Sometimes you must suffer right down to your roots. Plants exemplify human honour. You can only pull them up once. If you're strong enough, if you don't mind killing them, you must take firm hold of them, close to their roots. Pull once or twice and then let it go – that will help you find the best position. Don't rush it, take your time, treat the plant kindly, and yourself, too. When you're prising it out, you must take firm hold of the stem and pull it out carefully, root by root. When you hear the earth groaning, as if roused from its sleep, you will have opened – in this little, quaking patch of land, in the shade of this noble walnut tree – a hole that matches it in depth and breadth and darkness. The deed is done: you now have the roots of the yülerzik in your hands.

The roots of most plants look like new-born babes. But a yülerzik has a root as thick as a thistle's. You will see that this long and slender plant has unexpected depths, and a smell to match: strong, stringent, and quite heavy, too. Break the yülerzik's neck and wipe off the soil. Brush away the insects crawling between the tendrils; they're no use to anyone. Set the roots out in the belly of the sun and dry them for two days. You must stay with them. Do not fret if you scorch your lips, or scab your nose, or burn your ears. In the end, there will be nothing left of the yülerzik but a handful of fibres. What you do next depends on how good you are with your hands. Light a fire, for nothing but this. Make the flame rise high enough to cook its soul. Find yourself a reasonably clean iron sheet and set it over the fire. When it's red-hot, start roasting those roots. When they burn, you'll burn with them. Take care to watch its torn soul rising up with the smoke. You must partake of this fire, and this fate. As your nostrils burn with its smoke, as you watch the yülerzik recede beneath the ashes, you must never lose faith in its cunning. All transformations give out a bad smell.

Gather up the silvery ashes, taking care not to waste a single speck, moisten them with one or two drops of water, and begin to knead. As you knead the ashes, they will darken. A light fragrance will now begin to rise from the dough, and you'll have to hold yourself back to keep from tasting it. So this is what we call *aşkâr*. You'll have to keep kneading it until it has the right consistency. You must place it on the cleanest piece of muslin in the house and put it out in the sun for a few hours to dry. Then put it in a container and let it dry even more. It's different with every plant. You dry nettles, and the linden leaves you boil, and the yarrow you put in brandy. Each plant has its own whimsy, just as we do. A plant's secret lies in its healing properties, and its poisons. Even our least loveable angels have wounds that can be healed with a devil's touch. The important thing is what the devil shares with the wound. So if you can manage it, if a piece of *aşkâr* dough should fall into your hands, know this to be the yülerzik's small but precious secret. You now know how to find it and how to prepare it. In fact, all this is not so very important. What's important is how you decide to use it. To understand the yülerzik, you have to set out on the long road that leads straight to *aşkâr*. What a shame it is that we cannot tell you how *aşkâr* should be used. The truth is, we've already told you too much already… From here, it's up to you. You can stop, or you can carry on.

# Aşkâr

*For Adeviye Tuncer*

SAFE INSIDE THE SWIRLS of wood-scented steam, Canan stripped off all her clothes, tossing them into the driest corner. She had only just stopped crying. And now she turned the wood stove's little tap. Water went singing into the copper basin, splashing against its sides. Despite its untameable clutter, this primitive bathroom was Canan's only refuge from the noise outside. Here she could relax.

Sitting herself down on the low stool, Canan watched the steam rise up in anger, escaping the basin to draw her into its billowing cloud. Warmth, at last! Such warmth that she even forgot the tears burning her eyes. At once her cheeks reddened. Beads of perspiration formed in the little space between her flushed breasts. Most girls with breasts got to leave home, but no chance of that for her. Except now, at least, she didn't have to keep her legs clamped shut. She could let them fall open, watch the flower bloom. She passed a light hand – a very light hand – over her hair. Her plaits sat heavily on her shoulders, pressing down on her like hands. So now she undid them. Unlocked them and set them free. And soon they were tumbling down her back, and forming a skirt over her thighs. The ache of release. Deep inside her, something lifted. She rubbed her eyes. She yawned. She took a deep breath. And after that, she managed at last to stop biting her lips. Her eyelashes were sticking together, her eyebrows drooping. The thin line of fuzz travelling up to her stomach now resembled a black gash, drawn with a lead pencil. And so it was that the girl came fully into focus.

She readied herself for a ritual cleansing. She was imagining a long and peaceful slumber under streams of hot water, when in came Gülsüm. How dare she? Clanging and clattering like a dented teapot, or a saucepan with a broken handle, making more of a racket than that sewing machine she bashed away at, day in, day out. Bringing the chill in with her, as she strode towards her daughter. By now the water in the bowl was scalding hot. Canan had begun mixing in water from the cold tap. But Gülsüm wasn't having that. Gülsüm to the rescue. Lunging forwards, she turned it off. What on earth was she wearing? Bright white bloomers. A man's vest, going yellow. A muslin scarf, its lace edges unravelling. Almost naked, in other words. Almost naked... Canan, meanwhile, was almost boiling. So she sat up, bent over. Vertebrae by vertebrae, she raised her back above the water. Placing her arms between her legs, she braced herself for what she knew was coming next and said, in vain. 'The water's too hot, I can't take it.'

'You can take it. You *will* take it. You'll be fine.'

The bar of soap that Gülsüm now applied to Canan's small head felt as hard as stone. She rubbed and she rubbed, snorting as fiercely as if she were unleashing foul curses. Dipping a worn plastic bowl into the scalding water, she took the girl by the head and tipped the water over her. As the little thing lay there, covered in bubbles, still as a statue, the only places where the scalding water really hurt were her bruises, and the bites on her breasts. And how they hurt. She sat up. Where to hide, in this tiny bathroom? Just a little less pain, that's all she was asking. And simply wishing this was enough to lift her spirits. Turning towards her mother, she tried to look her in the eye, but the stinging soap bubbles got the better of her. She couldn't keep her eyes open. She just sat there, taking it, and it only made Gülsüm angrier to see her Canan turning inwards, taking refuge in her shell. It only fed her fury, and it was not just dirt she was beating out of her daughter, nor cleanliness that her daughter was so passively rejecting. For now, as Gülsüm scoured Canan's back with a loofah, the girl lifting her elbow from time to time, to brush away the strands of hair that were itching her forehead, she forced herself to say the unsayable, through gritted teeth.

'Tomorrow we are going over to Gülizar's, to pay our respects.'

And suddenly Canan was freezing, right to the tips of her fingers and her toes. She felt her mother's words tumbling through her, like jagged stones. She rubbed her burning eyes. She tried to open them. She wanted to look her mother in the eye. But she couldn't.

'I'm not going. Don't you go either!'

Gülsüm went back to work on Canan's back, almost slapping her with the loofah.

'That's out of the question, I'm afraid. If we didn't pay her our respects, people would talk.'

'Then let them.' She was overtaken by an urge to be done with it. To say it. She played with the idea, let the words form on her lips. And then she said it. '...so what if he croaked. Asım was a cretin, and now we're free of him!'

Gülsüm struggled to keep her composure and, conceding a little to her angry daughter, now added a tiny bit of cold to the scalding water. Setting the orlon loofah on her knees, she stared at the mountain of soap bubbles that rose as high as the cloud of steam, before brushing it off. She hesitated for a moment, then turned to her daughter's white back. Gently, very gently, she passed her hands over the places that had gone red from the rubbing.

'You mustn't speak against the dead like that, my girl. When someone dies, your anger must die, too.'

And now, as she picked up the loofah, to spread its silken bubbles over every inch of her beautiful daughter's body, with compassion and respect, and as she used the back of her hand to rub the soap away from the corners of her eyes, which were still squeezed shut, she was almost overcome with tears. So she straightened her skirt and tightened the knot on her muslin scarf. She had to stay strong. Keep her thoughts from wandering. Canan reached back to lift up her hair, piling it over her shoulders. She picked and pulled at it, and then she squeezed the water out of it, sending it streaming onto her knees. She took the small clump of hair that was left in her hand and threw it into the stove. It stank up the room as it sizzled.

'Why can't people speak against the dead?'

Gülsüm felt her chest constricting. She breathed in the steam, felt it seeping into her heart. 'Ahhhh,' she said, in a voice worthy of the great Asuman Arsan.[12] 'God will settle his accounts, my girl.'

Still soaping her daughter, Gülsüm paused to scoop up a handful of water. Through the stinging forks in her bloodshot eyes, Canan watched her mother splash it over her face. She had never seen her like this before; how bent and stooped she was. She was missing her eyeteeth. There was a huge crease in the middle of her forehead, from all that frowning, and her breasts rested on her stomach. Once upon a time, she'd had everything. Now, nothing. Nothing beautiful had lasted. Nothing but those agile fingers that flew about as if her fat hands did not own them. The tips of her fingers still had life in them, but every other part of her was falling apart.

'Father said… they knifed him, didn't they?'

'Yes. They knifed him.'

'Through the heart?'

'Yes, straight through the heart.'

'Were there any witnesses?'

'How were there going to be any witnesses, my girl? Apart from a few street dogs. It happened in the middle of the night.'

Again she felt her mother's full weight on her shoulders. She felt guilt creeping up her back, and disgust, and anger. She breathed in the white steam rising from the basin, the

12. A famous Turkish actress and film star (1934-1997).

black smoke rising from the flames, the sharp tang of soap and her mother's spicy sweat. She couldn't bear the weight. She made herself smaller, as once again the bruises on her stomach and between her legs began to sting.

'So you'll stop being angry at Asım?'

'I'll stop being angry.'

'And you'll stop crying all night long?'

'Stop making things up!'

The basin was overflowing. Dragging it towards her with a single hand, Gülsüm came level with her daughter's knees. Canan looked down at her mother's fat feet. She saw how firmly those fat feet were planted on the slippery stone floor. She saw how each of her splayed toes held onto it like hooks, and how those blackened heels crackled under the woman's great weight. She was seeing her mother for the first time, and she blinked. She wanted to sink into her mother's black well. She followed her, followed her scent. Smiled and cast a line. Caught nothing. Couldn't bear it.

'Mother?'

Throwing down the loofah, Gülsüm let out a wet sob. Pressing her soapy hand against Canan's mouth, she stared into her eyes. At last, Canan caught those twin fish that had evaded her for so long. At last, she could see the pain twisting from their tails. Gülsüm's nostrils were flaring, the knots of her muslin scarf loosening, and her undershirt was falling from her shoulders, to strip her bare. The veins on her neck thickened. On her temples there were two pulsating rods. The drops of water that had, until now, hesitated on her forehead raced down her face in fear, to fall off her chin.

'He's dead, do you hear! Dead and gone. Gone! So stay out of it, will you? Sit down, and keep your trap shut!'

What happened next was the scariest thing of all. Silence. Without pausing to test the temperature, Gülsüm grasped the handles of the bowl and tipped it over, to beat her daughter with water. For a few hot, desperate, airless moments, the girl thought her end had come. But still her mother pressed and pummelled and scraped until, like it or not, her daughter had been cleansed. And when Canan opened her eyes, it was to think for a moment of Asım, being washed on his slab – at this point, was there any difference between lying beside him, and not? She had no idea. For now, mother and daughter had finished their water fight to return to their own inner worlds. It was time for the *aşkâr*.

Gülsüm reached for a piece of muslin she'd put on the soap rack. Opening it up, she took out a black piece of clay. Breaking off a corner, she filled up her bowl with water once again and threw it in. As it dissolved, it sent out ribbons of coppery red through water that now glinted gold. While she waited impatiently for the clay to dissolve, she stroked her hips with her free hand.

'If those old biddies ask any questions, you say nothing, do you hear? Then when you pray, move your lips like you mean it. And even don't think of crying; that would only make them suspect something. Just remain impassive: no anger, no joy.'

Drop by drop, Gülsüm rubbed the *aşkâr* into her daughter's long, long locks. Gently, her fingers combed through them. How many long days since was it she had been this tender with the girl? As Canan's jet black hair slid through her lively fingers, it began to glow red, and cascaded down to her hips like a great silk road, declaring its independence, setting itself free. It rippled and it laughed. Twisted from side-to-side, while Gülsüm feasted her eyes. Such fresh beauty. How the red highlights shone. Her little gazelle, with her narrow forehead and her black eyebrows, her high cheekbones, her coffee-coloured neck. Her luckless lips. Her almond nipples. The curves of her groin. Until she had rubbed in the very last drop of *aşkâr,* she cherished her daughter.

By the time every hair on Canan's body had dried, night had fallen. The shutters had come down. From the pavements outside came the aroma of food on its way to the home of the deceased. For hours and hours, she combed her hair with the cherry wood comb she'd bought from Panayir. The day's heat was gone. Her feet were getting cold. She could feel the chill of night catching the ends of her hair, and climbing each hennaed strand like a cat burglar, until it flew around her face like a red mist. The strands lifted up, as if to share a joke, only to fall suddenly back into place, and because each one left an impression of itself in the air – a kind of afterglow – the room was soon swimming in red. Canan's hair was the pride of the neighbourhood. Its young men dreamed of running their hands through it, if only just the once. Canan reached up now… was it her hair she touched, or her head? After a time, it was probably her head she was touching. Little glints of gold spilled down her face, in silent conflict with the light in her coffee-coloured eyes, as ideas never before born and questions never before asked and possibilities never before considered took root in her mind. She took herself by the nape of the neck, as roughly as if she were catching a wild kitten by the tail, and ignoring the shrieking and the scratching, and the *aşkâr*'s mysterious lustre, she grabbed a fistful of hair, and with a snip of her scissors, severed it from its roots.

The dogs barked for a long time that night, and the gulls squawked as they flitted back and forth over the city dump. Next door, Feruzan's baby came down with a fever, and cried all night. At dawn, when the muezzin made the call to prayer, he coughed twice. As the city buses sent clouds of exhaust into the first light, Gülsüm rose from her bed with an unbearable itch. Suffused with *aşkâr,* the hair had woken up, and now it sat there, waiting.

# The Well of Trapped Words

AT NOON EVERY DAY I have to take three dishes over to my grandmother. Usually it's stewed fruit, pilaf, and potatoes with mince. My mother puts the containers into a nylon bag, and after she's handed it over (never forgetting to remind me how valuable nylon is, and how I should bring it back) she sends me off to my grandmother. Sometimes she throws a few apples into the bag, too. One is for me.

My grandmother looks like an apple herself – a shrivelled apple. Her hands are covered with freckles, her back is bent, her flesh grainy. To feed her we have to grip her where it doesn't hurt and sit her down nicely. Then we talk, but it's messy. She has no teeth, and while she's talking, she's also eating, so food keeps spilling from her mouth. She'll tell us a story for maybe the thousandth time, without changing a thing. I'm the only girl of the house, and that may be why, as I listen, I can almost taste the solitude that dooms her. I must be a good-natured sort of person; when my grandmother is telling me her stories, I open my eyes wide, as if I'm hearing them for the very first time.

She's always telling me about a snake. In the old days, the snake would slide into their stone courtyard and raise its head and hiss, and then, in a language no one was ever able to identify, tell a story. My grandmother, who was very small, could understand every word of what the snake said. Everyone else in the household, and especially the women, would scatter screaming, and that was why they never made the slightest bit of sense of the snake's strange hissing.

And I would say, 'Oh, please, tell me, what stories did this snake of yours tell you?' Even though I knew them by heart. I would ask that, and my grandmother's eyes would cloud over as she fell into a deep silence.

Then she would say: 'If you ever plan to kill a snake, I'm not telling you! I swear, I'll never tell you!'

According to my grandmother, the snake would come to the end of its story and turn to her and say, 'What we have heard is true, but only those who hear can know,' and then, as fast as an arrow – or lightning, or rain, or a river – he would slip across the stone courtyard and into the garden. According to my grandmother, the snake was under a curse. There was nothing more painful than to feel something that no one else could feel, to know something that no one else could know. It was more painful than the most painful illness and worse than the darkest solitude. That was why people living under this curse were so sad and angry. In their eyes, a small crowd became a big crowd, and every shadow grew larger than it really was.

Once, in the middle of eating, my grandmother tapped her temples with a crooked index finger and then tapped mine saying, 'If you are the only one who knows something, you're in trouble! You'll end up all alone, like me. You'll rot inside, but never die.'

When she said that, a cold wind seemed to rush through me, and I shivered. I already had an inkling of what she meant.

Today, when I was on my way over to my grandmother's, I thought of a new idea. As always, I stayed off the path, hiking instead across the low hills and the pastures of clover. It was the best way to go if you were alone, even if it took longer. Along the way, I saw things I'd never seen before. For instance, there was a walnut orchard, and at the bottom of this orchard was a south-facing wooden house sparkling in the sun, and right next to this house was a low, stone-covered well, and next to this well was a woman. She was pumping up water and pouring it onto the ground. I went straight over to the woman and asked for some water, even though I wasn't all that thirsty.

The woman lifted her head. 'No, you can't drink this water,' she said curtly.

I was so taken aback, I just stood there. She looked at me, smiling sweetly. Her eyes covered half her face, somehow. 'This water is unclean,' she explained. 'A snake's fallen into it.'

'Really?' I said, trying to recall if I'd heard anyone in the vicinity mention snakes.

The woman could tell how young I was. Or at least, that I was younger than I looked. Smiling broadly, she said, 'I've buried the snake, but if you're interested, there's a huge turtle I've just crushed, or perhaps you'd prefer to see a good-sized spider…' I clucked my tongue and told her I wasn't interested.

Then she invited me up to her patio, for a glass of delicious lemonade. There were clusters of bells hanging from the rods that held up the bower. I sipped the cold lemonade as slowly as I could. With every sip, I asked her a pointed question:

'Is this your house, Auntie?
'No, it's my father's.'
'What about the walnut orchard?'
'That belongs to my elder brother.'
'And the well?'
'The well is mine, only mine.'
'Where are they – your father, and your big brother?'
'They're gone.'
'Where?'
'Far away, to the big city.'
'Don't you have a husband?'
'No.'
'What about children?'
'I don't have any children either.'
'Don't you get bored here?'
'Never.'
'What do you do when you get bored?'
'I talk to the well.'

'Oh really; does your well know how to speak?'

'Yes, but it has a strange voice; it sounds like a moan.'

'Are you the only person it will speak to?'

'I'm the only one who can understand it!'

'How long have you been speaking to this well of yours?'

'Since I was a child. When I started understanding the sounds coming up from the well, I was a little younger than you are now.'

'Weren't you ever afraid?'

'Never.'

'Okay then, what does it tell you?'

She threw me a furtive look. I knew then that I must never repeat what she told me, but I wanted to push my luck, so I did what I could to keep the conversation going.

'So when snakes die in your well, do you get upset?'

'I used to, but not any more.'

'Have lots of snakes died inside your well?'

'Yes. Lots.'

When she took my empty glass, she peered into my bag. The food containers were still in there, and the insides of the bag were covered with beads of moisture.

'Who are you taking this food to?'

'My grandmother.'

'Who's your grandmother?'

'Esma.'

'Esma? Is that the Esma with all the snakes?'

'Yes! That Esma!'

'Goodness gracious. So she's still alive, is she?'

'My father says she's 97, but my mother says she's only 94.'

The woman's black eyes glittered with sorrow. For a time she gazed out at the walnut orchard. Her pupils kept darting this way and that. Then suddenly, she whisked up her skirt and stood up. When she did that, I was obliged to do the same, even though I had no desire to leave.

Stroking my back with her strong hands, she said, 'Give my love to your grandmother. Tell her that Nermin sends her kisses.'

'Will she know who you are, if I say Nermin?'

'Oh yes, she definitely will.'

'Fine. Then I'll tell her.'

As we came down from the patio, she gave my back a friendly slap.

'When I'm an old woman, will you bring me food, too?'

'If you'd like me to, I will.'

'Promise?'

'Promise.'

As I walked away from the walnut orchard, I didn't look back once. With each step I took, I was sure that the well woman was standing there watching me, until I vanished from sight. If you asked me why I didn't look back… Well, all I can say is that I didn't. I just felt as if my life would end in that place, no matter how long it lasted.

When I got to my grandmother's house, I found her hunched beside the garden door. She's so much shorter than she used to be, I thought. Her nightdress was trailing in the grass.

'Where have you been?' she scolded. 'You had me so worried, I almost died!' I took her by the arm and led her back to bed.

She gazed into my face. 'You're sunburned. So, tell me. Where were you?'

I shrugged my shoulders sulkily, and gave her no answer. She knew full well that I was not going to say a thing, so long as she was scolding me. I got my stubbornness from her. Casting a hateful look at the food containers, she told me to peel her an apple. I was the first one to give in and break the ice.

'Auntie Nermin sends you her love,' I said, relishing each word.

'Who?'

'I said Auntie Nermin. She sends you her love!'

My grandmother gazed at me emptily. 'Nermin? Which Nermin?'

'She said you'd remember her. She sent you her kisses.'

'That's nice of her, but I still don't know who she is.'

'She's young, younger than my mother.'

'Whose wife is she?'

'I don't think she ever married. She said she didn't have a husband or children.'

'So she never married.'

'You know who I mean. She lives in that house at the end of the walnut orchard.'

'In the walnut orchard?'

'In that little wooden house.'

'Oh, yes, the wooden house. So tell me. Does it have a well?'

I jumped from my seat in excitement. I told her everything, in a single breath. Every word I uttered brought another on its tail.

'There certainly is a well! And it's a well that speaks! Did you know, Grandmother, that well tells her everything. Its voice sounds like a moan. And there are snakes, she says… lots of snakes! When snakes fall in there, they drown. Then Esma pulls them out of the well and buries them. The well tells her everything! It even tells her the snakes' last words!'

This last bit came out all by itself. Without my even thinking it. Or maybe I didn't know what I was thinking. But suddenly I knew I had to stop talking. Because now my grandmother had opened her empty mouth to give me the biggest, sweetest smile. Suddenly, her cracked lips were smooth. I could hardly believe what I was seeing. Without lifting her head, she raised her eyes to the sky. She lifted up her hands, as if to pray. How funny she looked, with her toothless pink gums. But what am I trying to say here? Smiles are contagious, so I started laughing, too. When my grandmother laughed, tears spurted from her eyes. They didn't roll down her cheeks; they spurted. And her whole body shook. After I had helped her settle into her pillows, her laughter grew gentler. Once she had calmed down, she gave me a joyful look. But it was a strange kind of joy, heavy with sorrow.

Then she closed her eyes. Her hands were tightly clasped over her stomach. She let out a deep breath, a very deep breath, and just then her chest caved in. In a single moment, like a tree that's been gnawed by wolves, suddenly falling. And I just stood there. My lips were trembling so badly I could feel it all the way down to my hands. In the blink of an eye, the little body in the bed turned black, and then there was such a smell, I almost dropped to the floor. She was rotting fast. As her flesh melted away, I saw a skeleton. Such bones she had, like pearls, even though she had been dead for years.

# The Viper's Son

THE SNAKE CAME TO the most beautiful house in the village. The scent of Arab soap rose from its wet floors, laced with a hint of milk. The stone columns around the edges of the porch were smothered in untameable ivy; you could almost hear it whispering. Âzem, the son of the family, was two years old. He laughed at everything he saw. He had just one tuft of hair. His skin was as white as marble; his eyes like two pebbles, as he gurgled and laughed. His mother Zilver had parked him on a wooden bench, propping him up on both sides with pillows. He sat there alone, happy as on his mother's lap, trying to eat a bowl of yoghurt and instead smearing it all over himself.

The snake was a poisonous viper that sang like a bullet when it bit. It took its time. Slithering slowly across the porch, it was drawn by the fresh scent of yoghurt. Zilver was in the kitchen, boiling dried plums. And though they filled the garden with tart steam, the scent of yoghurt still found its way through.

The child was defenceless, as the viper slithered ever closer. A slip of a whisper was Zilver's answer to Âzem's burbling, but she did not know what he could see approaching: a snake. The lace curtains in the windows fluttered. The snake left behind it a trail of crushed grass. It climbed the wet steps and reached the child. First it sniffed Âzem's little feet. They smelled milky, rosy. The yoghurt was higher up, over the front of the child. The viper slowly raised its head. Shrouded in black, darker than the darkest depths of night, it slithered up on to the bench, and to the cushion next to Âzem. And this is when the whole world went silent.

The whole world. Even the birds stopped singing. Standing over the plums, Zilver suddenly noticed that the only sound she could hear was their bubbling. They were on the verge of brimming over, but Zilver went rushing out to the porch. Âzem, her handsome little boy! Naked except for his pants, which were as white as butterflies. He had mosquito bites all over his chest. In his hands, something black and monstrous… a strap, now where could he have found that? A whip, a glittering sword. Oh my dear God, a snake! Zilver let out a scream so shrill it echoed back from the mountains. And Âzem… The child was holding the viper by the head and playing with it. Squeezing it as hard as he could. Babbling happily, and drooling. He dipped his little fingers into the yoghurt and smeared it on the snake's mouth. Then he licked those fingers, as if they were covered in sugar. Turning to his mother, he held up the black creature for her to see, then squeezed the viper a little harder. The snake rattled and sank its teeth into its own skin. Zilver's eyes turned to ice, her jaw locked, her lips began to bleed as she silently moaned; only the viper heard her.

There she waited, as still as the village minaret, as still as the viper. The woman felt her legs growing longer and longer, until they were three storeys deep. She felt herself climbing up onto the shoulders of the village itself. She felt the mountain wrapping itself around her waist. But still she stood there, stiff and still. Âzem went on swinging the snake and winding it around him, laughing madly as he shook it. The snake was not able to raise its tail or climb up the boy's neck. Zilver began to cry. So did the viper. Each was grieving, in silent prayer.

Drunk from the pleasure of his holding game, the boy called to his mother, squeezing the snake a little harder, clenching it a little more tightly in his hot hands. Zilver was about to keel over, the viper too. The snake's spine stretched in agony, its muscles relaxed and it went limp. It could no longer hear Zilver's shivering cries inside its own breaking bones. And at last Âzem grew bored with his game, and let the snake go from his pincer-like hands. Falling to the ground, it looked no different from a length of rope. As it died, it let out one last rattle.

Bored with his yoghurt, bored with the snake, Âzem began to grouse. As fast as her feet could take her, Zilver rushed to his side. Picking up Âzem's spoon, she prodded the snake. She could not tell if it was alive or dead. There was a silvery light on the ground; a prince of the wells, embroidered with black pearls, a woman's voice, a fine winter's sleep; a giant viper, the most powerful creature in the village. She could feel the anger coming back, and the fury scratching her throat as she reached out and slapped her son across the face.

The boy cried so hard he nearly lost his voice. His eyes were wide with horror, his face smeared with yoghurt, and on the edge of his lips, a little drop of blood. Zilver picked up her son, shook him, and carried him up to bed. The plums had long since boiled over. The fire had gone out on the stove and the house stank of gas. She opened up the windows in the back rooms, and closed the door of the bedroom where her son was lying. Then she checked him, to make sure he hadn't been bitten. She wrapped her arms around him, dabbed his lips, wiped the tears from his eyes with her fingers, kissed the insides of his hands, and then ran back to the porch. The viper was still lying there. That's when she began to weep, furiously. Whatever she had inside her, she heaved it out. She tore off her muslin scarf. Tore at her hair. Swayed like a poplar.

She picked up the viper as if it were a gold chain. Embraced it like a sister. Felt the cold skin and took that feeling inside her. Shivered. Loathing rippled through her, and grief. With her skirt she wiped the yoghurt from the viper's head. She cleaned it and caressed it, as gently as if she were caressing her son's hand. When she could bear it no longer, she clutched her chest and said whatever prayer passed through her head, and while she prayed, she cried. Then she picked up the creature, suddenly heavy, and carried it to the blackberry bushes at the back of the garden and dug it a grave with a fine view. She laid it out straight, taking care not to squeeze it. Then she buried the viper, as carefully as if she were burying her own father, or her beloved mother. The viper had been wronged. As for who killed whom, and who gave his life to whom – only Zilver could say.

# The Well of Broken Places

IT HAD COME AS far as the steps, and was about to poke its head into the basil-scented courtyard, when it came eye to eye with a presence, half-man, half-mountain, long-legged, and bare-chested, with a beard the colour of ash.

The moment he saw the white snake, the old man jumped back in terror, but the snake did no more than curl up where it was. Inside each was the filament of a heartstring so fine it had never been seen or suspected until this moment, but now it had been plucked, to turn them into foes.

Now the snake rose, slowly and warily, preparing to strike. It was the purest white – how could anyone kill such angelic beauty? Clutching his axe, the old man fixed his eyes on the snake's neck. His palms thickened, as his lifeblood flowed into his axe.

As he raised his arm, the old man let out a hideous roar, striking the snake not just with his axe but with his voice. As the axe plunged into the snake's neck, two drops of blood fell onto the stone floor, and there they remained, never to be erased. These were the signs of the grudge the snake held against the world, and the debt to be repaid. It would perhaps have done the same as him, if it could: taking its time, rearing back, fixing on the red line of the old man's artery and flying straight at it, fast as an arrow, forcing its poison into the old man's bones, and with this one thrust, blackening his eyes. And thus they would have found him: splayed on the courtyard floor, a string of blood seeping from his lips, his fingertips turning purple. An unlucky death, but a clean one.

Nothing left but to say their prayers over his grave. It could have turned out like this, but it didn't.

Poking the snake's severed head with his foot, and hardly able to admit to himself his admiration for its lovely scales, he heard a scream coming from the house. A woman's scream, a mournful one: the girl they'd been expecting for some time had at last entered the world. He looked first at the house, and then at the snake. With his foot he rolled the snake into the bushes, and then he did what he had not done for the six scamps who'd come before her: he gave his new granddaughter a name that came from the depths of his own soul. Three times he uttered it. Three times he said the prayer to save her from the evil eye, and when the infant was brought to him in her pale swaddling clothes, he addressed her with false joy and gave her the name Sedef. Mother of pearl.

A few months later, the children found a coiled spine in the laurel bushes. When he was presented with the skeleton, the old man relived the murder all over again; taking it in his hands, he passed his fingers from bone to bone, as though it were a set of prayer beads, sighing his remorse, sighing and saying how sorry he was that it had come to this. Chasing off the boys who had gathered around him, he buried the snake, with long-due contrition. He had not killed an innocent, this he knew, but still he had felt that violent urge, still he had raised his axe to this snake like no other being, seized by an incandescent fury that knew no conscience. He looked suspiciously at the laurel bush; its honeyed fruits were dripping with anger, or so he thought, as he ripped the bush from its roots.

The spring rains began to wane, and how they waned. At first the fountains still gurgled, and the faces of those who drank from them were still tinged with blue, and the corn sagged under its own weight. But when, by summer, they were left with water as warm as blood, they would gaze up at the sky in despair.

A few years later, all that was left after the grasshoppers had finished munching was a great expanse of bare, cracked fields. Showing no mercy to those who had performed good works and prayed five times a day, paying no heed to hearts crushed by fear, ignoring the tears in the eyes of those whom the weight of holy words was slowly crushing, and making no allowances for the horned rams sacrificed in its honour, the drought descended on them all. As strangers will do when they happen onto such places, they would look up at the sky with wild and open-armed entreaty: Oh please, give us rain! But when they searched that sky, they could feel the anger in its closed heart: all that rained down from that flat blue firmament was resentment. From the red dawn stretching over the wasted fields to the cliffs beyond the ridge, the ragged earth wore the marks of its ire. It took even the dew from the rocks, turning it into steam and sucking it away. To make sense of the drought, people searched the arid expanse between clouds, and in the nightmares that came to them afterwards, they saw bloodshot eyes. It made no sense, not after all those prayers – how was it right to burn their lands with hellfire? Why had the sky vented its anger on innocent trees, why had it punished them with drought at just the moment when their seeds had taken root? As the face of the earth went on quietly cracking, the sky peered down into its deep fissures like a long-estranged brother. Drought – two things, born of the same blood: the embers are like eyes, and the eyes like embers. Deprived of water, people's eyes turn into embers, for it is in embers that fire finds its essence. Impelled to protect the soul – the thing inside us that is in greatest need of water – they could hardly hear themselves begging, their burning souls: Please give us water!

When saffron-yellow scorpions of eight segments requisitioned their rooms, first the men left, then the wives who could not bear to be apart from them, then the frightened, hungry mothers-in-law. At dawn the elderly prayed for rain, flitted between shadows, swore never to leave their land. Those who stay are always the proud ones; those who leave, the martyrs, have no choice but to break away from a future of known cycles; having succumbed to uncertainty, they prepare themselves for whatever might come. The people who remained did so with hearts grown smaller, beating for just one drop of water. Just one drop of water would be a miracle in seven colours.

Sedef grew up, and when she was ready to speak, her first word was 'grandfather'. At first he meant no more to her than the great calloused hand that stroked her head day and night. In time she noticed a pair of soft eyes behind the hand. There was no doubt she was close to this grandfather of hers, but each time he hugged her, each time he took her in his arms or lifted her to his shoulders, she felt strangely troubled. When she peered into that broad-bodied man's ears, she could see the dark passages that led to his conscience. But she could no more understand her grandfather than she could the notion that water had once existed. In Sedef's innocent mind, her grandfather was the thirst itself. Grandfather was drought.

It wasn't long before she worked out that the grandmother who carried her here and there, like a basket, was not her real mother. For Sedef came to life by ripping through another: as she took her first breath, her mother took her last. Above all, she was born in the same moment that the snake had died, and this became another bond between herself and her grandfather. Death and salvation, terror and curiosity, this girl and her grandfather had lived through these twinned moments. Both had the smell of death on them.

For the sombre reasons above, the cord between Sedef and the old man grew steadily stronger, and the more it grew, the more tangled and potent it became. Whenever she could, Sedef would scratch her grandfather, and bite him, and pull his hair, and twist together strands of his beard. Her grandfather would play with the child until she hurt him, and – his patience spent – he would slap her, leaving her alone in the courtyard, wailing. They neither loved or hated one another quite enough, and on evenings when the dust had settled, people would see a scarecrow racing across the cracks in the earth; an old man imploring the sky, and running behind him, stumbling and falling, rising and staggering, but never flagging, a small girl.

Some years later, when the old man finally accepted that the firmament was deaf to his pleas, he took up his knife. Sedef watched on, entranced. The way his hand gripped the knife, the strength of his wrists, and in his eyes, that fire of determination, and oh, those puffed cheeks, those bulging blue veins. A sudden jolt, and the child jumped back. She realised just then why he had always appeared as a blur to her; she had only ever seen him knifeless. Stiffening, she looked sadly at her grandfather, as for the first time this bearded body came fully into view, and a confused memory floated through her mind, leaving the residue of death in its wake. Sedef did not know what she was remembering; as she looked at her grandfather, she could not define what she was feeling. Grandfather walked swiftly over to the apple tree, which had been parched by the sun. He inspected the branches one by one, until he found one thick enough to grasp. He took a long time breaking it. Pulling off its dry leaves, he at last wrested the forked branch from the trunk. By the time he returned, Sedef was long gone, safe in a hiding place where no one could find her.

It took her grandfather a whole day to sharpen the branch. As the earth baked under the sun's angry rays, it swam with hazy images. He whittled the branch, mindless of the grasshoppers' infernal chirping, or the way his world was slowly turning yellow and crumbling before his eyes. When he held up the black branch, stripped of its bark now, to become his lucky staff, his spirits soared, and he lamented all the years he had spent abasing himself before the earth with all those broken little pleas. Why had he not thought of this before – he, who above all, was the master of wells. Instead of bowing to the sky, he was perfectly capable of proving himself a prophet and finding water with a simple divining rod.

Towards evening he brushed the shavings off his knees and raised up the divining rod. In his hand he held all human faces and all things: this was his image. He went to bed, forgetting the onyx prayer beads that had never left his side since he was a young man, and in his dream that night, he saw a full moon; oblivious to the laws of the planets, the moon bowed down in all its nakedness – down so low that it touched his forehead.

The night passed, and from then on, he arose each day to scour the earth with his staff, moving his head as carefully as a full jug, holding it high enough to see the world at eye level. His homeland spread beneath his feet; his hope, a black speck pressed against the horizon. He would sway across the earth with the confidence of a prophet, tapping the ground as he searched. The moment the staff quivered, however feebly, he would stop, listening to the sounds around him and separating out each one, until he located the faint trickle of running water coming up from the depths. Wherever the rod's fork took him, there he dug. If he hit a big rock while digging, instead of taking umbrage he would simply work around it. When he was sure there was no water, he left a great pit behind him and moved on. Before afternoon, he would return home covered in dust, bent over double with backache, a sad imposter of a grandfather. The man who made grand statements at breakfast, railing against all who passed before him, would by evening be sipping his soup in sullen silence. For months, he dug here and he dug there, and by night his sleep was broken by moans from the pits he dug. Yet he still clutched his blessed divining rod close, to answer the night, to rebel against it, to resist; as the tumbleweeds danced he would vow to find a deeper well, a much deeper well. Clutching his shovel, he would dream of a prophet snuggled beneath the earth, an old man, a holy man, his face shining with light. Even if he clenched his teeth and strained his mind, he could not place his own eyes on that old man's face. He slept fitfully, crushed by the might of another being, of whom he told no one. And until she heard him breathing steadily, Sedef didn't sleep a wink. And so it was that the wells gazed out at two sleepless people.

It was a quiet, listless autumn day. Sedef stood in her grandfather's doorway, listening to his tired snores as she waited for him to wake up. Her eyes were brighter than ever, and her childish scent had spread to all parts of the house, like a lily fully bloomed. Naturally, her grandmother had not noticed that the house was much quieter than usual. Biting her lip with an eagerness she found unable to hide, Sedef opened the door just a crack to look at her grandfather. As the stillness of morning floated in through the narrow window, casting its blue light, her grandfather, so exhausted from digging, had spread the fug of sleep around the room already thick with his dust. Sedef crept in, as quietly as she could. Fearing that her own heartbeat might awaken him, she held her hands to her chest. When she was level with his head, she gazed at his face, slack with sleep, and marvelled at how big it was, then stood there helplessly, daunted by a head so large. Her grandfather's hand had released its grip on the divining rod, and now lay under his pillow. Sedef reached out with the tips of her fingers and gingerly gripped the divining rod. He began to pull it slowly, as slowly as if she were tugging at a split hair. It was as if she could see it for what it was now: this rod, born of the drought and the day of the fearsome knife. The drought was an illusion reflected on the face of a man who had pockmarked the earth, guided only by an ordinary staff.

When her grandfather woke up to find that his divining rod had vanished, he went into a rage, rising in a frenzy to hurl himself outside, clad only in his pants, something he had never done before. Sedef had broken the divining rod into as many pieces as her strength had allowed; shivering, she awaited her grandfather. When he saw it reduced to worthless splinters, he went after the child, raging. Sedef managed to jump out of his way, and when she saw there was nowhere else to go, she vaulted the low wall and ran over the cracked fields, as her grandfather gave chase, roaring loud enough to make the stones crack, too. There was no road, and his legs felt as though they were about to break. He told himself that he'd been expecting something bad from this little devil all along, because of how brazenly she'd gazed into his eyes, her own eyes unlit by conscience, and when he scolded her, she would never bow her head, but look straight at him!

On Sedef ran, and just as she was about to be seized by the scruff of her neck, she felt the shadow of his powerful presence looming over her, a presence so fearsome she knew she must escape it. Panicking, she wheeled off to one side, and then to the other, leaping the bushes that covered the wells, and each time she twisted her ankle she stumbled to her feet again, refusing to give up. By the time her grandfather caught her, the child was all torn up. Her knees were grazed, her elbows scraped. She'd struck her chin on a stone and her neck was covered in blood. She was still panting when her grandfather clouted her on the back of the head, pushing her forward. Fierce with pride, Sedef tried not to cry. After giving her backside a slap or two, her grandfather pulled her up by the arm; the child swayed about like a ragdoll. Sedef rubbed the cut on her chin, and her grandfather took out a handkerchief, and moistening it with spittle, he cleaned the wound. After this small act of mercy, Sedef mumbled a few tearful words: that she knew where the water was, she had seen this water in her dream the night before. Thinking she was mocking him for his own dream about the prophecy, he shook Sedef hard. He could not bring himself to be addressed in this way by so small a child. He spat on the face of the scorched earth: you just wait and see what I have in store for you when we get home!

No, grandfather, she said. If she was lying, may she wear her shame before the world. But an old man with a beard the colour of ash had come into her dream, holding a silver shovel. And he'd said, when your grandfather wakes up in the morning, tell him to give up his forked rod.

Her grandfather swallowed hard, and looked the child over. All her muscles were tensed, and he could see no trace of a lie on her split lips. But how it grieved him, to hear that he had entered his grandchild's dreams wearing another old man's face; even as he took in the good tidings, how it grieved him.

'See? Look over there, just behind that black boulder, a well dug there would yield enough water to last 40 years.'

Dragging his feet as if he'd not heard a word she'd said, he took Sedef home, throwing her into her grandmother's arms, and telling the woman to get her washed and her wounds cleaned. He sat in the courtyard smoking, until next morning, and as the black frost chilled his bones, he mentally settled accounts with the luminous old man who had invaded his grandchild's dream. Clearly he had wanted the freshest and most innocent consciousness. He had let him carve up the fields like a fool, while others looked on in puzzlement. Testing his faith like Jacob, perhaps. And then, to finish him off, he had used a girl's lips to tell him that the staff he'd carved so lovingly was useless.

At dawn the next day, he set off with as pure a heart as he could muster. Eager once again to dig, he looked for the rock Sedef had pointed out to him. The moment the shovel hit the rock, he could smell fresh earth, and so it was that, with a concentration he had never known before, he went on digging. The more he dug, the deeper the old man sank into his hole, until soon he was removing boulders the size of his own head. From time to time, he submerged himself in the maddening silence, straining his ears for the sound of water, and even though he didn't hear it, he kept on digging, and the more he dug, the greater the distance between him and the sky. Towards noon, grey clouds began to sink towards the ground, carrying with them a sweet breeze. But he knew nothing of those clouds, or that breeze; he was still shovelling earth at the bottom of his hole. As the sky darkened, he heard a bang, a flash of lightning, a clap of thunder. He stood there, like stone, so deep inside that hole that he could see only a sliver of sky through a jagged gap. Unable to believe the drops hitting his face, he stared at his wet hands. He fell to the ground. There was nothing, now, for him to take home. He was as empty as a snakeskin. Quelling his lament, he gathered all his strength. He tried to pull himself up the side of the hole, but he couldn't manage it. Slowly the water flowed into the land; little by little, it filled the many holes he had dug in the cracked earth. He tried to call for help, but how was anyone going to hear him from that distance, as they rejoiced in the rain? And who knew where the well was, aside from Sedef? It had been her prophecy; she might come back. Might come back. His mind went blank, as providence rained down on him and, eyes still open, he began to weep.

# The E in Elif

IT'S THE MIDDLE OF the night, let's say. There's a new-born baby in the house, and the fragrance of its sleep is wafting from room-to-room. Proud to have become a grandmother at such a young age, Neriman is listening to the baby's heartbeat through her fingertips, while a stray moonbeam lights up the little girl's face. She's only ten days old.

Let's say that – following fierce discussions involving all the family's branches and generations – this baby has yet to be named. Neriman goes to the room where her daughter is in confinement and shuts the window. As she flutters about, smoothing the bedclothes and plumping up the feather pillows, preceded everywhere by her round belly and huge breasts, she calls to mind a dove, or a cloud on tiptoes. Let's say that Ahmet Bey is just drifting off into sleep; an old man's sour, yeasty, perforated slumber. He doesn't even hear Neriman coming back to bed. To clear his throat, he looks up at the ceiling and coughs twice. Then he sets about scratching the sores on his chest.

Murmuring sweetly, Neriman tries to pull Ahmet back from sleep. Let's say that Neriman has something she wants to say to him before he drifts off. But then, there's always something she wants to say.

'You're not asleep yet, are you, Ahmet,' she says gently. She hesitates, as if anxious not to bother him. When he doesn't answer, she turns noisily in bed, pressing her huge breasts against Ahmet's hairy back. 'Shall I bring you some hot milk?' she asks. 'It might soothe your throat.'

Ahmet strokes his chest: he has heard her rosy murmurs, but in not answering he has made it clear that he wants to go back to sleep. So Neriman tries again.

'Would you like that hot milk, then?'

'No, I wouldn't. Now go to sleep,' says Ahmet. But beneath his imperious words, there's weakness.

Let's say Neriman has something to discuss with him, something best left for a moonlit night. Ahmet doesn't know this, but – as trifling as the matter might be – she's thought about little else all day. She's been waiting for everyone to go off to bed, for the house to fall silent. Through that long wait, she has been thinking up little sentences, all beginning with the words, 'Let's say'. And making sweet dishes, the sort that keep you awake at night. And strong coffee, for the same reason. And she's smiled more than she's needed to. Trying to look happier than she felt.

'It's been ten days, and we still haven't given this girl a name,' she says coyly. She places her plump hands on Ahmet's aching stomach and begins to stroke it. 'Our visitors keep asking.'

At last Ahmet turns his garlicky breath in her direction. Struggling to keep his heavy eyelids shut, he speaks through his nose.

'What choice do we have, with everyone interfering?'

Pulling up the blanket to cover Ahmet's shoulders, and tucking it in, Neriman says, 'That's all well and good, but it's up to you to name her. She is your first grandchild, after all. And you're the mother's father.'

Ahmet stops to think for a few moments. As the whites of his eyes flit about like fish, he utters a name: 'Fine, let's call her Ayşen, then. Ayşen's a lovely name.'

Let's say Ahmet has already given in by the time Neriman catches his innocent sentence by the tail.

'Ayşen,' she says. 'Well, you know best, but you do know that Ruşen gave his granddaughter the same name.'

'Which Ruşen?'

'The Ruşen from our old neighbourhood, the one with the furniture store.'

'He has a grandchild?'

'He has, yes. He has… That's what I heard.'

Ahmet still doesn't realise that he has wandered into one of night's snares where Neriman lies in wait, raising her slender eyebrows, offering up answers with ambiguous questions concealed inside them. He pulls at the elastics of his pyjamas. Let's say that when Neriman sits up, propping herself up with feather pillows, she knows that Ahmet is now going through a list of names.

'In that case,' says Ahmet. 'Let's call her Gül. It's the name of a flower, and it suits her.'

'Gül?' says Neriman. 'You mean you are going to name your grandchild after that slovenly Gül? Don't you remember how much we argued with her last year?'

As he remembers Gül's shrill screams, Ahmet's face goes sour. Putting his hands behind his head, he tries to look like someone who is thinking more clearly. In the end he just stares at the ceiling.

'Fine, then. We'll call her Selvi. Selvi! We'll name her after my dear departed mother.' As his voice reverberates through the bed, Neriman lets him know that she has bowed to it.

'Selvi. Yes, that's a beautiful name, certainly. Fine, then. You can let everyone know, first thing in the morning.'

Thinking the matter is settled, at least in Neriman's mind, Ahmet feels some relief as he pulls the blanket up to his neck. At this point he murmurs, *Selvi… Selvi…* Neriman waits for a minute or two, listening to Ahmet's breathing. Then she wrinkles her nose, and asks an innocent question. Or at least, a question that seems innocent on the surface.

'Selvi is a rather old-fashioned name, don't you think?'

Let's say that Selvi is Ahmet's final decision. He is running out of patience, and beginning to get angry.

'What's wrong with Selvi? It means long and slender. Like a cypress.'

'Fine, but what if the girl isn't tall? We're all short in our family.'

In exasperation, Ahmet starts scratching his chest again. He keeps thinking, one eye closed.

'Fine then. Let it be Oya. That's modern enough.'

'But what if her friends teased her?'

'Why would they do that, woman? Why would they do that?'

Burying her head in her pillow, Neriman looks up with fearful eyes. Or at least, eyes that seem so. 'Why are you shouting, at this hour of night? You'll wake everyone up.'

Wheezing, he gets up and takes a cigarette from the top of the bedside table. Neriman doesn't like him smoking in the bedroom, but this time she says nothing.

'Whatever I say, you find some excuse to shoot it down,' he says. 'Why on earth would they tease her for being called Oya?'

Neriman answers with sweet timidity. She hasn't been afraid of Ahmet for a good five, six years now.

'Oya, Oya, Oila, Oil Paint. That's what they'll say.'

Ahmet sucks in his cigarette as if he's about to eat it. Then he coughs. Three times. Let's say the poor man is sick and tired of having to deal with the maze of his wife's mind, just to get the simplest thing done.

'Damn it! This brainless woman is keeping me from thinking straight. I can't think of a single name now!'

Stroking Ahmet's shoulders, her voice sweet with sleep, Neriman now speaks. 'Never mind. You'll find the right name tomorrow. Come on now, put out your cigarette. Let's go to sleep.'

After Ahmet has put out his cigarette and got back into bed, he gives Neriman's legs a harsh push. To make it clear that he is done with speaking, he turns his fat stomach to the edge of the bed. Nermin is left with no blankets, so she quietly pulls them back. 'Ahmet, do you remember that teacher lady who came to the house all those years ago? Saliha. Do you remember her daughter?'

'So what if I do?'

'Well, you liked her a lot, I remember. What a bright woman, you said.'

'Yes, yes I did.'

'What was her name. It was something beginning with 'e', but... Dear me, what was it?'

Ahmet waits a few moments before turning back to Neriman. Brandishing a fist, as if to punch the pillow, he spits out a threat.

'Are you trying to keep me awake, woman? Tell me, so that I don't do something to keep *you* awake!'

Later, Ahmet's sleep mixes in with the snores and whispers of the household. The longer he sleeps, the stronger his smell. Let's say that with the help of the moonlight, Neriman watches him sleep for a time: his grizzled face, his white eyebrows. Then she quietly shuts her eyes. Her lips curve in the knowledge that tomorrow will be a new day. As always, she drifts off by screwing up her face and counting the things that are in the refrigerator, waiting for breakfast.

The night ends, and with the clear light of day, the house wakes up. Soon it is alive with the morning's clamour. Once again, Neriman uses her clove tea to get everyone to the table at the same time. And now in comes Ahmet. He is rubbing cologne into his freshly-shaven face. It stings, and his eyes are bloodshot. Everyone stops talking. His son-in-law hides his cigarette in the palm of his hand while he stares at the potted plant next to him. His daughter, immersed in womanly concerns, has taken out her swollen breast to feed the baby. The baby's father rearranges himself to shield at least part of the breast with his hand. In the hope that Ahmet's first words will not be directed at him, he averts his eyes. With heavy steps, Ahmet walks across the room. Extending his great hands, he strokes the baby's head. He raises up his head, as if to deliver an edict.

'I am naming my granddaughter Elif. And that's the end of it. There is to be no more empty talk about names in this house. Do you hear?'

Then he moves to the head of the table, where he stares down at Neriman, as if from a throne. Neriman is standing next to the steaming teapot. She brings it over to the table. As she serves them all tea, the steam curls its way across the table, laughing.

# Lost

AUNTIE FEYMAN WAS a nervous sort of person, even when she was thinking of nothing besides the nails she'd just painted. We gradually got to understand this side of her; slowly began to see through her. Her nervousness, and the rollers in her hair, and the way she would suddenly appear in the stairwell looking like a ball of dough in that robe of hers, only to come back a few minutes later looking like a film star, wearing net stockings. She probably didn't mean to agitate us, but she did. And to top it all off, there was that creepy laugh of hers. It sounded like someone ripping thick cloth.

Feyman was doing her usual that day: while the other residents of the military compound were dressing for the ball, she was tearing her hair out and racing around, crying, 'I can't find Suat anywhere. This time the child really has gone missing! Or, maybe… could he have run away?' All this, while making sure nothing touched her newly painted nails.

Suat was always hiding. It was nothing new. But that day, Feyman was really in a state. Before she started screaming and pulling the place apart, she'd searched the basement, the canteen storeroom, and the treehouse in the back garden, so we knew that Suat really was missing.

Suat was all eyelashes. But instead of making him more handsome, it made him look as if he was carrying two hairbrushes over his nose. I realise now why I never warmed to him: I could barely ever see that kid's eyes, or how he looked at things, or even what colour they were, most probably because he was always looking at the ground. Not even at the ground – mostly he just looked right through things. Even when we were having lots of fun, on our way to the beach, for instance, or a picnic, or in the garden, playing dodgeball, Auntie Feyman would suddenly cry out, 'Our Suat has gone missing again, children. Oh please, could you help me find him,' and the fun would be over.

The first few times this happened, we actually enjoyed looking for Suat. It was like a game of hide and seek, only more exciting. But when he began to make a habit of it, we stopped enjoying it. So on the day in question, when Auntie Feyman told us that Suat was nowhere to be found, again, we all ran off to our houses, because we were fed-up with having to look for him. Then, when the grown-ups couldn't take Auntie Feyman's shrieks any longer, they sent us back out, to search the gardens and the stairwells, the guardboxes and the boiler rooms, but when we called out, 'Suuuuuuuuaaaaaat, Suuuuuuuuaaaaaat,' you could tell from our feeble voices that our hearts weren't in it. And this time, we couldn't find him.

Auntie Feyman used to think she was wise to his tricks: the boy couldn't bear to be away from his card table, next to the camellias in the back garden, for long. When Suat (who always, in our eyes, seemed rather dirty), got bored and suddenly vanished from sight, it was understood that he would probably reappear by night fall, and Auntie Feyman wouldn't make too much of a big fuss of it. But the week before the ball, when he disappeared as usual, he was still missing at dusk. You should have seen the state Auntie Feyman was in. Her hair was standing on end, as if she'd been electrocuted. She tore around our neighbourhood until she collapsed. In the end, we found him crumpled up in the space just beneath our balcony. Or rather, my mother found him.

He was cold, his eyes were gummed up and his nose was full of snot; you can imagine how frightening his bushy eyelashes looked. There were even a few ticks in his hair. My mother gathered him into her arms at once and carried him into our house. When Auntie Feyman saw the ticks, she let out a cry of pure disgust, and pushed Suat away. She wouldn't even put her arms around him. This scene upset my mother very deeply; you can tell she's upset when her lips droop down at the edges like that.

It was five in the morning by now, and we were all fighting sleep. Our happy-go-lucky fathers had already gone off to bed; when you passed certain doors, you could hear heavy snoring. Everyone was tired of this game of Suat's, too tired to be upset anymore. The boy had caught a bad chill, with a hacking cough. Of all the people gathered around, only my mother's lips drooped. When I saw her sad eyes searching the room for me, I flew to her side. She took one look at my bare feet and my flimsy nightgown, and took me into her arms.

I thrilled to her voice: 'You're going to get a chill, my child!'

Her lips were still drooping; she still looked on the verge of tears. How I hated Feyman for upsetting my mother! Suat, too! And his ghost of a father! I wrapped my arms around my mother's neck. There was Suat, sitting silently in his chair, legs crossed, appraising us, giving us a rare glimpse of honey-coloured eyes. How envious he was, and how angry! I snuggled up to my mother a little more when I saw that. More than a little! Suat glared at me and I glared back.

But now, what did my mother say but, 'Why doesn't Suat sleep here? Then I can clean him up.' I burst into tears at that point. I thought my veins would explode from jealousy. My mother frowned sweetly, waiting for me to calm down. But I kept up the stubborn crying, and tried to cover my mother's face with my hands. Even though I couldn't say I didn't want Suat with us, my mother knew full well that I didn't want her to squander her love on Suat. And now she used silence to teach me that I was going to have to accept this. All this as she gently passed her long fingers through my hair.

In the morning, my mother lit the stove in the bathroom and gave Suat a good clean. When the noise woke up my father, he scolded her for trying to look after all the messed-up children in the world, and that reassured me a little. But still, I was burbling with rage, just to hear my mother murmuring to Suat, and so when I couldn't get back to sleep, I went to sleep next to my father. He stroked my back with his giant hands. Two strokes, and I was fast asleep.

As the week wore on, Suat seemed to think he'd found himself a mother. He was at our house day and night. He'd come over for any reason at all; even if he just felt thirsty. With every new day, his eyelashes grew longer, or so it seemed to me. Each night, I prayed to God to be delivered from Suat.

'Oh, great God,' I would say in my deepest voice. 'I beg you to deliver me from this maniac Suat! My mother feels sorry for him, and that makes her love him, and the more she loves him, the closer they become. If this keeps going on, she's going to forget all about me.' And then, I would sob and sob in bed, as if the worst had already happened.

Just when all the grown-ups had begun to say that Suat seemed to be straightening himself out, and wasn't going missing anymore, he did it again. Worse still, it was the night we were supposed to be going to the ball, which everyone immediately forgot about; I was left like a baby doll, in my new pink skirt, while everyone went off to look for Suat.

What I love most about summer nights are the fireflies. When there are fireflies, you don't fear the night. So I joined the search, and we looked everywhere – in the brambles at the back, in the beach huts on the shore, in the canteen storeroom, in the boiler rooms, in the stairwells of the apartments, beneath the stairs. But the earth had swallowed the boy up.

While everyone was still running around and calling out his name, I began to retrace the day in my head: we'd come back from the market on the noon bus. Feyman had put an apple into Suat's hand, and off he'd gone to his card table, eating the apple as he went. Then me and the other girls had started playing with our spinning tops. I couldn't recall seeing

Suat anywhere. After that, I'd gone home to get a drink. The door had been open (for the last few weeks, my mother had been leaving the door open, because she was tired of children ringing the bell). The pressure cooker had just been taken off the stove and was still hissing steam. I'd poured myself some water and gulped it down. I called for my mother, but there was no answer. At first I thought she wasn't home. That made me very happy: the place was all mine! I went into her bedroom, to play with her make-up, and there she was, curled up in bed and fast asleep. A light cover was draped over her bare legs. She wasn't wearing her nightgown – she was just napping. Without making any noise, I went outside again. Now I thought about it, I was pretty sure Suat hadn't been around then, either. He must have been missing since the middle of the day, not just since dusk. Something struck my heart, and my eyes began to water with fury.

The mothers did their best to calm the hysterical Feyman, while some of them whispered amongst themselves about what an irresponsible woman she was. Some were still wearing their fancy ball gowns, but they couldn't find it in themselves to board the busses. How could they think of leaving Feyman Hanım[13] in such a state? Some of the fathers did. Protocol, they said. They had no choice but to be in attendance.

I couldn't see my mother anywhere: that must mean she was still out hunting for Suat. I ran back to the house. My father was lying on his bed, reading his newspaper, oblivious to the commotion outside. His formal attire was hanging on the outside of the wardrobe. First I snuggled up to him and told him a few funny stories. I asked why he hadn't gone to the ball. He hadn't really wanted to go anyway, he said. After that, I slowly slipped off the bed, like I was playing a game. My father continued reading the paper, with great concentration. After a while, I slithered underneath the bed. There wasn't much room down there. The only source of

---

13. A respectful honorific appended to women's first names.

light was a creepy pair of eyes, beneath a pair of brushy eyelashes. I thought: there's no escape. Suat brought his finger to his lips, asking me to keep quiet. And I did. I kept quiet. That's all I can remember.

# Sorrow Hunter

1

I'M NOT AS TALL as Nilüfer. Whenever we sit side-by-side on a bench, my legs are left hanging, until they start swinging back and forth. It takes so much of my attention, all this swinging, that I'll try crossing my ankles to make them stop, but when Nilüfer goes off into one of her stories, they start up again. And then half the things I say to Nilüfer come out sounding like lies. If a person is going to talk straight, they have to sit straight, don't you think?

We're in the schoolyard. The other children are scattering fast. After my last talk with my mother, I know what I have to say, and I give my words a lot of thought beforehand. I'm being brave, but my actual words are as soft as chalk.

'So listen, Nilüfer… Come for an hour's walk with me, from the market to the park; we could do it every day.'

'But when I walk my legs rub against each other. I get a rash on my calves.'

'Can't you walk with your legs open?'

'Don't talk nonsense, and don't expect me to walk like a boy who's just been circumcised!'

Her crazy similes cheer me up.

'Listen, how much do you weigh these days?'

'Promise you won't tell anyone?'

'I promise!'

'Promise on your brother's life.'

'Why him? I hate my brother.'

'If you don't swear on your brother's life, I'm not telling you!'

'Okay, I swear on my brother's life that I won't tell a soul.'

Nilüfer looks warily into my eyes. 'I've changed my mind,' she says.

I pat her on the back, to reassure her. 'Never mind, if you don't want to tell me then you shouldn't,' I say, 'but you have to go on a diet right away, you really do.'

'If you only knew how many times I've tried that. But when I see what everyone else in the house is eating, I can't stop myself. Vegetables in oil, meatballs… I get so hungry I can't sleep at night, and then I get up and gobble things down.'

'Do your parents know you do that?'

'They must do, but they never say anything.'

I lean closer to Nilüfer's face. I use my firmest voice, like I'm giving her a warning. 'This has to stop, Nilüfer! You have to be disciplined. Your family has to help you! Because if it goes on like this, you're never going to get thinner!'

Her face crumples with frustration. And I feel bad to have said something that she's heard hundreds of times from other people.

'Oh, stop. Please! Please don't feel bad. You're beautifully fat! I mean it, really… But down the road, before you reach 30, even, there are so many health hazards. High blood pressure, diabetes, and things like that, not to mention indigestion…'

Joining her fat white hands, she rests them on her lap to gaze hopelessly at her fingers. Beneath her thick lashes, her eyes mist up with sorrow.

'No one wants me to get thinner.'

I hold her hands, but she won't hold mine. It's like a kiss not returned.

'Don't talk nonsense!' I say. 'How could you even think such a thing? If you ask me, you haven't managed to convince them that you *want* to lose weight. I mean… What I'm trying to say is, your parents don't even know how determined you are to get thinner. Do you see what I'm trying to say?'

She pushes my hand off her lap.

'What are you trying to tell me, huh? I'm a child. They're the parents. You're mixing things up, aren't you? They're the adults!'

For a long while I don't know what to say. To tell the truth, I'm a little angry about the way she pushed my hand away. I'm the only one in this school who talks to her. If I get up now and go, she'll be all by herself. One huge ball of navy blue, kicked away into the playground dust.

'Darling Nilüfer,' I say in my softest voice. 'Listen, you're getting everything wrong here. Our parents aren't growing, in actual fact. You're the one who's growing. You must never expect them to be cleverer than you are.'

She frowns and glances at me in shock. I can tell that she can't understand what I've just said to her.

'Parents do everything they can for their children!' she says. 'Everything!'

'Okay, then, but what if they don't know what to do?'

'How could they not know? They know what to do, but they just don't feel like doing it.'

'What do you mean, exactly?'

'What I need is a private clinic, do you hear? A place with lots of fat people like me in it. Dieting and walking just isn't enough! We'll all eat the same things, and get up at the same time every morning, and do sports, and liposuction…'

'Are there really places like that?'

'Of course there are; I read it in the newspaper only the other day. There's this private clinic that's just opened in Balçova.'

'And so? Why didn't you show it to your father?'

'I showed him, but he didn't pay any attention! Places like that are very expensive, apparently.'

'But you people are rich…'

'Not us people, just my father!'

Jumping to my feet, I plant myself in front of Nilüfer.

'Why don't you go to Ege University Hospital? Our upstairs neighbour Auntie Gülseren went there, and she lost 30 kilos in a year. It's cheaper there, so your father will agree to it for sure, just you wait and see. If he doesn't go for it, I can speak to my father and he can try and talk him into it. My mother could speak to your mother. I don't know, we get down on our knees, maybe, and beg. His heart isn't made of stone, after all. And then, I could visit you every day you're in hospital. You'd lose a year, but what's a year? It would be better than suffering like you do now.'

Nilüfer looks back at our school. With a face like a storm, she crushes all my hopes.

'I'm not going to that hospital!'

'But why?' I ask impatiently. There's some contempt in my voice, too − I'm that sure of getting a stupid answer.

'My brother died in that hospital.'

'You had a brother who died?!'

'Yes, and he was only four, a little four-year-old golden-haired bundle.'

'What happened? Why?'

'We don't know. First he had this high fever, and then all we could see were the whites of his eyes. That's all I can remember now. The whites of his eyes. What colour eyes did he have, I wonder?'

## II

My mother is angry with me for being late home from school. She has such a soft heart, she can never speak to me harshly. But she still subjects me to a never-ending torrent of questions. This time I want to tell her the truth, the most important truth of all. But she just won't give me a chance.

She's just taken out her curlers, and while she talks, her curls keep bouncing. She's going out soon, to a tea party, and that's why she's so nervous. I notice how pale her face is. It's yellow, almost. I like seeing my mother so worried about me she goes this pale. I hold my tongue, to make her worry even more. But there's something strange in the air – anger. It's coming at me from my mother, and after it hits me, it fills up the whole kitchen. I don't understand why, of course. I've been late home from school before, but she's never looked at me like this. And so now I'm beginning to get worried, too. My mother seems to want to say something to me, but she can't find the words. Then suddenly they fly out in a puff of air.

'Do you know what anal sex is?'

'*What…?*'

'Are you saying you don't know?'

'I don't even know what you're talking about.'

'You didn't hear about it from one of your friends?'

'Nooooo.'

'Now you listen to me, Serpil. Tell me straight! Have you ever heard about anal sex before, or haven't you?'

'But Mum,' I sob. 'I don't even know what those words mean!'

My mother leans over me, darkening me with her shadow. As she speaks, she keeps making new shapes with her slender fingers. She's trying to be as frank as she can, to fend off further questions, but because she can't manage this, she keeps jabbing herself. She keeps talking about an 'inverse relationship', and blushing. What I mean is, this is the only thing she says during all that mumbling that I can even begin to understand. Without meaning to, I screw up my face. When she sees me shudder at the thought of an 'inverse relationship' she calms down a little. Her face begins to look a little less flushed.

'If you ever hear one of your friends talking about things like this, ask me first, do you hear?' she says. 'I can explain things better.'

'Fine, but where did all this come from? No one's talked to me about anything like this.'

'Not even Şebnem?'

'No, she didn't.'

'Now you listen to me carefully…' My mother wags a finger at me. 'I don't want you spending any more time with that Şebnem!'

'Why not?'

'That girl has run away from home so many times already, and I hear that her father was beating her. She's had to grow up too soon, that girl, and she's from a blood-thirsty family, too, so I don't want you ever going to her house again.'

I'm confused now. 'I don't understand, what exactly did Şebnem do wrong? If I was getting beaten all the time, I'd run away from home, too.'

My mother jumps back in horror. 'Are you saying you think it's a normal thing, her running away from home?'

'Yes. Everyone knows how many times she's run away from home. And every time her father finds her, he takes her to be examined, to make sure she's still a virgin.'

My mother's eyes grow large with terror. 'If you knew all that, then why didn't you tell me?'

I hang my head and say nothing, because I'm too little to stand up to my mother when she's shrieking her head off like this. Picking up the dishtowels, she throws them back down on the counter. 'That girl was taking men home and having inverse relations with them. Just look what kind of life this girl is leading, and at such a young age! You are never to see this Şebnem again, do you hear? On no account are you to see her! If she comes to you, then you tell her – you tell it to her straight. Say your mother won't let you! If I see you with Şebnem, or if I hear you're meeting with her secretly, even once…'

In a meek little voice I say, 'All right.'

She looks deep into my eyes, as if to weigh the sincerity of my words. I look right back at her, and use my eyes to write it across my forehead in giant letters. ALL RIGHT. Are you convinced now? My mother calms down. She looks a little sorry, even, to have shouted at me like that. Without another word, she puts a bowl of soup in front of me. I'm feeling full, but to make her happy, I wolf it down. My mother watches me, and calms down a little more. But her eyes are just as anxious. I am still chewing on a piece of bread when I say, 'I've found a new friend, anyway. A very fat friend. I hardly have any time left to think about Şebnem.'

# Stolen

RIBS! FOR MORE THAN 60 years, he'd lived a clean life, and now here was the fate that had been written for him. His life reduced to a pile of bones, wrapped up in a dirty cloth. That was all he could see now: a worn and brittle thigh bone. A collar bone protruding from a lifeless body. A shrinking ribcage, caging his soul.

He didn't have the slightest desire to get out of bed. It had been days since he had washed his face. He'd spent those days gazing at the mirror's wise pronouncement – his own two ruined eyes – and listening to the soft sighs of the damp and peeling wall. He was no longer praying for a dry bed in heaven, or the empty depths of a velvet night in space. It was enough for Zeynep not to see him like this.

If there was one thing he was sure of, it was that he'd die alone. But he was also sure that when they heard the news of his death, all the children he'd clothed, the girls he'd settled into marriage, the boys he'd fed and sent off into work would come from all four corners of the country to stand beside his grave. He was a man who'd never extended his hands to be kissed, never judged a man by his shy lips without first taking the temperature of his forehead, and yet, to his marrow, he had felt all the warmth of human obligation. Once he was dead he would not, of course, begrudge visitors who wished to stroke the marble stone, or fall to the ground in tears. He was, to the best of his knowledge, the world's most benevolent man – the merciful King İlyas, looking out through the concave glass of the fish bowl. When the acrid fumes of death had finally overtaken him, he might appear, momentarily, to bow to defeat, but once dead and buried in the humble marble tomb they'd erect for him, he would regain his kingdom. So long as Zeynep did not come to see him.

As he turned onto his other side he felt the sting of bedsores on his back, which were the size of hands, and propping himself up on his elbows, using all the strength he could muster, he slowly pulled himself up. He shuffled towards the window in his scuffed leather slippers. Halfway there, he was caught by a coughing fit so painful it seemed to dislodge his ribs. It ripped his throat, punched his stomach, and roared through his head.

Leaning on the windowsill, he watched the afternoon sun pierce the dust. It was early still. He could never get himself comfortable before evening. For 20 days now he had been breathlessly, so breathlessly, marking the minutes of sunlight, hoping to die before Zeynep visited. Every evening, as he listened to the world heading home, he would pine for the grey hues of dusk; every night he would implore the angel of death to take him before he had to face another day. He'd not seen Zeynep since he sent her away to her older sister.

Telling himself that he was worrying needlessly, he inspected the street. He watched the youths who were gathered in front of the shop that sold gas canisters, and the people going into the water depot, limping under the weight of their bottles. None of them caring if he lived or died. At the crest of the hill leading up to the main road, he spied an immodest young woman, lost in thought as she made her way down. Her hair was cropped short. Her long-sleeved blouse was the colour of burnt coffee. Low-heeled shoes left her ankles exposed. It took him a few moments to realise this was the blouse he'd bought for her – Zeynep! She'd chopped off her hair, without so much as asking for permission, and her long neck was bare for all to see. And how cheerfully she walked, as excited as if she was about to embrace the whole neighbourhood, her face lit up by a enigmatic smile, the food in her bag surely leaving behind it a steam perfumed with spice and oil. Still only 21. Still a child. When she walked, you could see her plump legs, her ample, bouncing curves, and a back that she kept perfectly straight despite the weight of the shopping. As she came closer to the house, grief coursed through him. Grief and terror. Swaying unsteadily on his feet, İlyas pressed his face against the glass.

It was a year earlier, on a sunny day like this, that they'd married. From the moment she'd walked into his house, with its odour of stale bread, she'd lowered her eyes as though afraid to pry, asking only where the bedroom was, and there she had carefully removed her travelling dress and gone to work. With her little hands – no strangers to labour – she cleaned the house from top to bottom. İlyas had gone out and bought whatever food they might or might not need. Goat's cheese, lamb chops, dill for some reason, fresh kidney beans, seven kilos of watermelon, bananas, hot chocolate, Coca-cola, nuts, and coffee… Whatever he thought the girl might never have tasted, he took back to the house.

During their first evening meal together, neither said a word. Zeynep kept throwing sidelong glances at the meat grilling on the stove. İlyas guessed the smell of meat and butter was making her light-headed, and served her a lamb chop in the hope that she'd open up a bit. Zeynep pinched it between her delicate, sparrow-like fingers and raised it up to her face – as though threading a needle – then gnawed it solemnly, right down to the bone, before very slowly laying it at the side of her plate. How cheering it was to see such poise, such pride, such determination to hide her hunger. Evidently the girl was too ashamed to ask for a second lamb chop. He waited for a few moments as she tried to clean her oily lips – dabbing at them with the tips of her fingers – before putting another chop on her plate. And then another. Little by little, the girl ate her fill. And the more she ate, the fuller İlyas felt, too, as the world itself seemed to grow in volume. How graceful she was. There was no rush, no hint of urgency or appetite as she chewed each morsel, and, now and again, lifted her eyes from the plate to look into İlyas' eyes, smiling with gratitude for the food and for the long life it would bring.

Zeynep was not particularly pretty. Her mouth tilted to the left. The dark mole on her cheek was awkwardly placed. Her thick eyebrows were set low, shading her eyes and obscuring the light in them. And yet there was something about her that alluded to feminine beauty. Her hair was long, hinting at luxury, as though oblivious to the scrawniness of her body. İlyas meditated on this as he watched her eat. You'd expect such a dishevelled girl to have lifeless, straggly hair, but Zeynep's hair glowed, as though the light that burned inside her escaped through it. Hair could instantly betray a person's hidden soul; a few clumsy strokes of the scissors in the clammy hands of someone who didn't know his business, and a face became twisted and lop-sided. And yet it always sprang back from its roots, relentlessly growing until arrested by death. There it was, that veil, rising up again, to seize life by the throat, a feast of curls around a shapeless face, flying free, never settling, offering easy sanctuary, camouflaging sin and vengeful thought, forgiving all trespasses, stopping time itself with white dreams of romance. Stranger still – even after death, the hair kept growing for a short while. Was it to prove that there was such a thing as a soul? It kept growing, to the eternal surprise of those who washed the bodies.

Yes, thought İlyas, Zeynep's face is made beautiful by her hair, standing defiant against any misfortune that might befall her. He hurried away from the table, lest he should submit to the urge to reach out and touch it.

Left alone with the bones and the crumbs, Zeynep blushed at the thought of what was to happen later that night. She washed the dishes, trying in vain to remember the advice her older sister had given her. She couldn't envision the caresses of an old and freckled hand, the moans, the thrusts inside her, the grabbing of her flesh. She could only imagine a dark weight on top of her in the darkness, and bearing that weight until at last it shifted and she could slip from underneath it and drop off into a deep, deep sleep.

Aching with fatigue, she went into the bathroom, removed her clothes, and lathered her scrawny body in preparation for their first night. Then she climbed into bed and waited, clammy and fearful in her floral nylon nightgown. She concentrated on staying awake and on trying to distract herself from what was about to happen, alert to the slightest sound coming from the sitting room. After some time, when İlyas had still not emerged, she began to feel annoyed. She felt a pain sharp as a knife, somewhere deep inside her nose, and though she had no desire to cry, she buried her mouth in the pillow and began to sob. Presently, a shadow appeared in the frosted glass of the bedroom door and İlyas approached, dragging his feet. From this slightly bent and depleted shadow there now came a soft, sweet string of blandishments.

'Don't cry, my girl. How could I think to deflower a girl your age… a man like me. It wouldn't be decent! The thing is, you're poor… when I die… because I will die one day, as we all will… this house will be yours… and my savings, too. You won't need to depend on your elder sister, you won't need anyone… Don't cry, my girl.' There were other things İlyas would have liked to say, but there was no point in saying them, not if he couldn't look her in the eye. It was late. Zeynep was tired. After listening to her sobs for a few minutes, he withdrew into the dark hallway.

Zeynep lay there, open-mouthed in disbelief at what she'd heard. Now he was gone, her body relaxed a little, but as she settled into the cotton bedsheets, she looked up at the ceiling and felt her heart growing smaller. Because what was the difference between being with a man awaiting death, and dying with him? When she punched the air in anger, she hurt no one but herself and the night.

Zeynep could not be described as a talkative girl. She would answer whatever question she was asked with a curt yes or a curt no, and then she would fall silent. Whatever İlyas asked for, she brought to him, and then she would return to her room to listen to the radio. This had not been İlyas' plan. He'd been hoping for a girl who nestled at his feet like a cat, casting fond looks at him. But this girl wouldn't change the tablecloth, or plant flowers: like the country girl she was, she pushed all the furniture against the wall, leaving the centre of each room empty. She lined up all the household objects according to size, establishing a haphazard and meaningless symmetry, and that was all. Although there wasn't a fleck of dust in the house (the whole place smelled like a wet cloth), neither were there any new dashes of colour; no beaded ornaments or pouches tied with satin sashes, or plastic ivy, or gilded trinkets. She brought not the slightest change to İlyas' dirty yellow desert of a life. Sheer ingratitude.

In the beginning, she wore long-sleeved clothing, but then she began to loosen up until she was flitting about in sleeveless tops. That hair she'd kept tightly braided – she now let it fly free. She was still a child – yes, she was – but she carried with her the bitter sweat of a desiring woman, and took to bathing whenever she could. She loved water. Had there been any intimacy between them, he would have called her his water bird. No chance of that! Whenever he so much as said a kind word to his grim-faced, cold-hearted, plastic-lipped bride, she cowered in silence. If she noticed his kindness, she didn't show it.

On one of the coldest days of the winter, the house again filled with steam. Overcome by the aroma of soap, İlyas finally succumbed to his devils. Slowly, he rose to his feet and approached the bathroom door. He had second thoughts, almost turned back, then changed his mind again. He pushed open the door, just a crack, and beheld a naked form sitting on the wooden stool, like silk, smouldering silk. A shape covered with soap bubbles, translucent, rounded, and extravagantly curved, shimmering in the steam that could not quite erase it – half woman, half person. Her wet hair cascaded down to her hips. A birthmark just above her waist stared straight back at him, like an eye. İlyas was trembling, but he felt no shame (he was never ashamed about things no one else could see). In any event, he felt his strength waning, and didn't linger. He was old enough to know, even as he admired those breasts, that charming navel, the labyrinth below, how poisonous they could be. And anyway, this had never been his plan. He had married her not because he desired her, but because he pitied her.

He was just about to close the door when Zeynep felt a draft of cool air and shuddered. It was as though she could feel his terror-stricken eyes on her. Slowly, very slowly, she turned her head. Then she turned the rest of her body, to look straight into his eyes, as if to say *come in, have a taste*. She opened her mouth, as though preparing to bite him, and then – languidly, ferociously – she smiled.

From that day on, İlyas lived in confusion. He simply could not make her out, and his biggest fear was that she understood *him* perfectly. Such was the force of her character that İlyas felt himself slowly being pushed into a corner. She shamelessly went about conquering first the bathroom and then the kitchen, because she was a big eater, this Zeynep, the kind to put out four kinds of marmalade for breakfast. The meals she cooked for them lacked for nothing. They were well garnished, and there was always a pudding. Never once did she ask him what he might like to eat; she just went off to the market to buy whatever caught her fancy, and cooked it with incredible care. Same thing the next day. And as one day followed another, she began to swell up, like a violet leaf shimmering at the water's edge. He couldn't see her bones anymore. Her knees and shoulders were well rounded, and her narrow waist filled out. Her forehead broadened, her cheeks fattened, the mole on her face shrank and shrank until it vanished altogether. When she plucked her eyebrows, the curves of her eyes became more visible. As the sallow girl turned into a fleshy, ivory-skinned woman, İlyas felt himself grow ever smaller.

He envied her appetite, and would get up in the middle of the night to raid the refrigerator like a child, wolfing down all the fresh food he could, but what a shame it was that his stomach would begin to ache after just two or three bites, and he'd have to go back to bed. While Zeynep wandered brazenly about the house, he would watch her furtively, searching her larded body for some sign of oily excess: something hanging, swelling, thickening, some ugly sign that exposed the girl's shamelessness. He couldn't find it. From head to toe, Zeynep was unabashedly upright, faultlessly robust. She had not been there long, and already the entire house smelled sweet and pungent, amid clouds of flour and spice. The smell of food. Or was it the smell of Zeynep herself, which only those who saw her could enjoy?

In fact, it made perfect sense, this insatiable hunger, after a childhood in which she'd known only boiled potatoes and bread smeared with tomato sauce. That said, there was something ritualistic about the way she cooked. Instead of just throwing all the ingredients into the same pan and tossing them around, she worked as attentively as if she were on a cooking programme, selecting the ingredients with care, weighing them, washing them leaf-by-leaf before cooking them, then decorating the dish with sprigs of parsley and tomato slices, until it seemed almost untouchable.

İlyas had never asked for this. It was vanity, fully cooked. She must, he supposed, have realised he was the kind of person who didn't much care how things tasted, and these dishes of hers seemed to steam with unspoken resentment. Every time he ate, he suspected he was about to be poisoned. His appetite dwindled, and started fading. First his face caved in, with his cheekbones sticking out so much they seemed about to break through the skin. The skin on his neck became more deeply wrinkled. His stomach sank inside him, his legs became two twigs. He was a sick and feeble old man. He always felt tired. Sometimes his head would spin; when he walked about the house, he had to lean against the walls with his hands; when drinking water, it was a struggle to swallow. One night, during a furious coughing fit, he convulsed so violently it seemed to lacerate his stomach. He buried his head under the pillow, trying to muffle his coughs so as not to awaken Zeynep, sneezing with his mouth shut, and swallowing hard – anything to quell the itching in his lungs and to stop coughing.

Zeynep appeared at his door in a white nightgown. She peered through the night like an angel of mercy. In a voice that was softer than the moonlight on her face, she asked if he'd like something hot to drink. Unable to stifle his cough, İlyas tried to shoo her away. Zeynep came into the room. Gently, very gently, she began to stroke his chest. Something full of goodness, and as warm as blood, spread across his torso, and İlyas saw the trap into which he had fallen. He could see Zeynep's eyes in the darkness, their glint as sharp as lightning bolts. In these eyes, now surveying his own wretchedness, he recognised the emotion that had until this day been his most intimate companion. It was pity, mercy from on high – that destructive compassion that landed like a millstone on those too weak to resist it. He pushed away the girl's hand, prodded her with his foot to make her go.

As soon as his raking cough subsided a little, his thoughts turned to freeing himself from Zeynep. No sense waiting until daybreak; at night it was easier to hide how weak he'd become. He rose from his bed, shaved himself, combed his hair, put on a woollen vest that would keep his back warm, and when he was sufficiently spruced up, off he went to find Zeynep.

His voice was hoarse, his eyes bloodshot. He began to recite the words he'd memorised. She must leave at once. There was a better way than this. She was young, too young to be shut up in a house all day long, she deserved to be out gallivanting instead, he would send her money. Once he was dead she could return to the house, and that was a promise, but right now, Zeynep had to leave. Soon he would die, as did everyone, sooner or later, but he was going to die alone, because it was a shame to keep a girl her age inside… And so on and so on.

Zeynep stood there dumbfounded, clutching a teapot. When he'd said his piece, she frowned and made rather a performance of hesitating between speaking and saying nothing. Yes… but that's impossible… what would people say… well, you know best… did I do something wrong?

The more she said, the worse he felt. She thrust a few things into a bag and left the house. For 20 days, she'd not picked up the phone, nor come to visit. After outstaying her welcome, she'd left him to savour her absence. All İlyas wanted was to die before she came back, but the fear that she might return at any moment kept his heart racing, and that kept him from dying.

Now, as he set eyes on his little wife sauntering down the hill, he resolved not to die so long as Zeynep wished him alive. How happily she walked. She smiled at the youths idling in front of the water station. She stopped. She answered their curious questions at length, showing them the bag in her hand, then glancing up at İlyas' window. İlyas shuddered and drew back. He took hold of the net curtain, to stop it fluttering. He caught a glint of the gold chain around her neck, saw how she gesticulated too much when she spoke, and shifted from one foot to the other too much, and shook her narrow shoulders when she let out a peal of laughter loud enough to shake the windowpanes. Then she continued slowly on her way, heedless of the fact that these youths were undressing her with their eyes. She stopped at the vegetable seller, and bought a cucumber without even bargaining. With a shattering self-confidence, she called out greetings to distant passers-by. Joyful, coquettish, bursting with life.

As she approached his door, she looked up at his window once again. Though she could not see İlyas through the net curtains, she looked straight into his eyes. İlyas went into a panic. He tucked in his vest and pulled up his pyjamas. His heart was beating as fast as Zeynep's footsteps as she skipped up the stairs. He tried to straighten his hair. He drank a sip of water to clear his sour breath. A key in the lock, the door flying open.

In came Zeynep, as cool as a night breeze. İlyas shuddered. With false concern, she said, 'Now what are you doing, standing up?' She quickly slipped off her shoes and put her bags on the counter. With a great show of pity, she surveyed the ribcage standing before her, the desiccated thighbone. 'Sit down! Sit down! Why are you still standing? You've lost so much weight. And your eyes – they've sunk into your head. I can hardly see them. You were wrong to send me away.' There was excitement in her voice, the kind you couldn't stand up to. She ran off to the kitchen, returning with a spoon. 'I made all sorts of food for you; it'll bring you round in no time at all. Enough of this letting yourself go!' She lifted the lid from a pot, releasing the fragrant aroma of chicken broth, slightly over-seasoned with pepper. Kneeling in front of İlyas, she brought the spoon to his lips. İlyas was unable to speak to say no, but tried to clamp his mouth shut. As sweet as she seemed, the sparkles in her eyes were like splinters of ice that could not be melted, even by the smile that played across her lips. İlyas was on the verge of tears; his nostrils quivering, his forehead reddening, his chin shrinking. She was trying to bring him back from the dead. Again, she lifted the spoon. In her eyes, he saw a furious wish to embody the munificence that had begun to eat itself away, even before his body began to rot. She shoved the spoon into his mouth, all the way to the back of it. He had no choice but to swallow. What he couldn't swallow dribbled down his chin. Still staring into İlyas' indignant eyes, she picked up a napkin, and with compassion he could only call theatrical, she wiped the soup off his chin, and the saliva from the edges of his mouth.

# Women's Voices

B WOKE UP IN a sweat, troubled dreams still seeping into her hair, her mind all over the place. The bedroom was airless and smelled of sleep. She stretched out her right leg, opened herself up, just a little, like a pair of rusty scissors. Then, impatiently, she turned onto her stomach, and unable to breathe, onto her back. Whenever she began to doze, there was her own breath, like a stale story, and she was awake again. She thought and she pondered. Whatever she had been thinking every morning for the past four months, she thought it again. She rolled herself out of bed, cracked the window open without drawing the curtains, and a gust of cool air rippled across her chest, bringing with it the noise of the street. She slipped on her dressing gown, inside out, but instead of fixing it, she just did up the buttons on the inside. The shiver in her chest abated somewhat. She looked at the phone. She thought of lighting a cigarette, but didn't. She thought of running a brush through her hair, but didn't do that either. She picked up her little notebook and sketched herself a tiny woman – long, thin and dark. Then she jotted down a few little sentences, neatly at first, but the faster she wrote, the larger the letters, and the more they tilted into the margins. Her handwriting had never been any good. She'd always written down her thoughts like this; quickly, letting them find words for themselves. It was as though they weren't thoughts at all until she could see them on the page.

She looked at the phone, at its cord, all in knots. She untangled the cord and blew away cigarette ash that had fallen between the phone's buttons. And now she was holding the receiver and punching the buttons with the tip of her pencil, with no idea how the number had drifted into head. Her voice would still be gravelly from sleep. She cleared her throat while the phone rang, so brashly. If no one answered by the third ring, she was hanging up. She didn't want to wake her if she was still asleep at this hour.

A stared at the ringing phone. Who on earth was this? At the second ring, she wiped her wet hands on her knees and rushed over. Her voice was dry and faint.

'Hello?'

*Shrill voice,* thought B. *She must be short, with small eyes.*

'Good morning, madam. I'm calling you from the İstinye Women's Union. We're doing a little research to find out how happy women are with family life. If you agree to answer a few questions for us, we can offer you a steam iron as a gift.'

Ay was afraid of strangers. Her shyness made her awkward. She had the habit of saying the first thing that came into her head, and so most people took her for a bit of a dimwit. Her mother-in-law had little time for her, and she was no longer on speaking terms with her husband's sisters. Behind her back they called her rude, common and ill-bred, though in fact they rather envied her looks. She had grey-blue eyes, and ivory skin, and lovely long hair, and in fact a coarse word had never passed her lips. Oh, but her voice… It was shrill enough to break the back of every word she uttered. It was a voice that belonged to an ugly face. Whenever she spoke, her hair got shorter, and her face darker. A huge whiskered mole formed on her lips. When she cried, she rasped like an iron gate. When she was angry, she hissed like a goose. When she made love, her voice strained so hard, you'd think she was trying to push out a turd. And when she was startled? Well, that shriek of hers could rip right through the Earth's core. This did not help her fear of strangers, especially strangers asking questions.

'Who are you? Who gave you my number?!'

*How coarse her voice is. She mangles her vowels. And she mumbles.*

Be propped her elbows on the dressing table. To keep from stammering, she averted her eyes from the eyes in the mirror.

'I dialled your number at random. Don't worry, I'm not going to ask for your name or address. All you need to do is answer my questions.'

'Oh really? Then how am I going to get my iron?'

For just a moment, Be could feel her heart in her throat.

'You can come and pick it up from us yourself, or you can send someone else. Whatever you wish – you know best. Maybe you could give us a postal address; that would make it a little easier for us... or we could meet somewhere... if that works best for you.'

Ayş tried and failed to brush off the dandruff that had fallen onto her shoulders. Her hands were still wet. She let herself slide to the floor and leaned back against the wall. Crisp little bubbles of sound rose up through her throat. She took a deep breath, and felt a little calmer, though her heart quivered with sweet anticipation. Why not, after all? A little interview would set this day apart from the others. She'd finished her cooking and the boy was at school, and so what if she didn't get around to sweeping the house today?

'Okay, fine, let's talk then.'

*She took her sweet time! Take it easy, now. Keep it cool.*

'Oh, thank you. So let's get started. How old are you?'

A lock of hair had fallen down over Ayşe's nose, and she swept it back where it belonged. Now there was oil all over her fingers.

'I'm 32, but people say I look younger than my age.'

A vicious smile formed on Berna's face. She bit her lips. *So she's five years younger than me. Hair as long as a dancer's, I bet. She probably bleaches it with peroxide.* 'People say I look younger than my age!' *Hah! She has fat arms and legs, this one, and a gob so big that when she smiles it's like a massive black pit, right in the middle of her face.*

'Are you married? Do you have any children?

'Oh yes, of course. I have a son. He just started school this year.'

In a voice that was as false as a forced smile: 'How lovely… Is there an age difference between you and your husband?'

'Not really. Well, my husband might be three years older than me but if you saw him, you'd see what a young face he has. He looks like a boy, really. I'm the one who has to shave him, even.'

*Quite the little neighbourhood hussy, I bet. No idea how to behave. And shallow, I don't doubt.* Reaching over to the silver cigarette box on the night table with the lion's legs, Berna took out a long cigarette. With a light heart she slid it into her silver cigarette holder. The taste of cold metal brought a smile to her lips. Nothing ignites disdain like the flame of comparison.

'Do you find him handsome?'

'Would I sleep with him if I didn't? I fell with love with him, didn't I? I married him. Although… Sometimes, I don't know, I sometimes give him the once-over and… I mean he's not one of your dark and handsome heroes. And he can be a little spoiled, to be honest, and he's picky about food. If he steps on a stone floor, he gets a stomach ache, and if he sweats, he comes down with a cold. He's a child, in other words. He needs constant looking after.'

'So what you're saying is that most of the domestic responsibilities land on you?'

'My husband works in the logistics business. He works all hours, as you can imagine. So the shopping, the housework, the boy's homework – all the drudgery falls to me. He gives me a weekly allowance and leaves me to it.'

'So he always comes home late at night?'

'Mostly, yes… In the beginning I used to stay at the window, waiting for him to come down the street, but I don't do that any more. The moment my head hits the pillow, I go to sleep. I don't even hear him come in.'

*Or does he strip and climb into bed, and snuggle up against her, while she's asleep? Does he slide his cold feet against her calves, or breathe in the scent of the little hairs on her neck, as he caresses her stomach? Does he cherish her stretch marks?* Berna's stomach began to burn, her chest prickled, her heart ached. She bit into her hangnail and tore it off, and the pain concentrated her mind.

'So you're saying he doesn't... neglect you?'

Ayşe let out a wild giggle. *If a stranger's on the phone, if you're talking to strangers, you shouldn't...* 'How could he neglect me? I open my eyes at night sometimes, and he's already on top of me. Sometimes I think I'm still dreaming.'

Berna broke her cigarette in two. She wiped her mouth. Her hands were shaking. She let her fingers travel across the nightstand, drawing circles inside circles, a mysterious shape, lurking in the whirls in the wood. Everything that lived left a trace.

'So your sex life's pretty good, by the sound of it.'

'It's okay. I mean, we do it like about four times a week or something. Oh, this is getting a bit rude! Shame on me!'

*Hah! That's enough, she's bullshitting me.* 'But what about you?' said Ayşe. 'Does it, you know... happen for you?'

'What do you mean? I'm not sure I understand.'

'I mean, do you experience orgasm?'

'...Yes! Yeah, of course!'

The sweat on Ayşe's hands had cooled by now, and for the first time she noticed how much the house smelled of bleach. She thought sadly about her numb fingertips. She felt so brittle, like she was made of ice, an ice statue. She tried and failed to feel some fire inside her, to heat up the rest of her.

Berna, meanwhile, had decided she could do with a strong coffee. She basked in her anger, as it opened leaf by leaf – like an artichoke, almost – and now wanted nothing more than to put down the phone. Even so, it was with some reluctance that she uttered her closing words.

'Well, thank you for your answers, you've been very helpful.'

'Was that all you wanted?'

'Yes, madam, all I need now is an address so I can send you your iron.'

'Forget the iron.'

'Don't you want it?' said Berna.

'Forget it, okay? I already have an iron.'

'OK, fine then, have a good day.'

Ayşe got back to her feet to hang up the phone. But then she paused. She stared at the receiver, as if hoping for a glimpse of the solemn voice that had left its story half told. How lonely she felt, how desperately she longed to escape this damp room, this stink of cheap soap, if only for a moment. How guilty she felt for saying all those things. How to make up for it? She saw her chance, and she seized it. *She's a cultivated, educated woman, I guess. What a soft voice she has.*

'So, tell me, are you married?'

This caught Berna by surprise. *So off we go, hand-in-hand down the road of no return…*

'No, madam, I'm not.'

'You never married?'

'I did get married seven years ago, but…'

'Why did you split up?'

'Please,' said Berna. 'The rules of our organisation prevent us from giving out any information about ourselves.'

'Did he cheat on you you, this husband of yours?'

'No… It was nothing like that. I was the one who wanted out.'

'Who looks after you now?'

'I can look after myself,' said Berna.

'You didn't have any children, I hope?'

If only she felt able to hang up.

'No we didn't. We couldn't.'

'Was that why you split up?'

'No, it wasn't. It just wasn't working out. Over time it just dried up.' *Okay, enough of the questions.* 'Madam, I'm afraid I have other people to call now.' *Bug eyes. That's what she has.*

*And such short hair, as short as a boy's, and why all those glass beads strung around that neck?*

Ayşe frowned, as her brow furrowed. 'You're just calling people up for the fun of it!'.

*Her voice is getting coarser and coarser. What a weird woman she is.*

'What? What makes you say that?'

'It's obvious, you're just calling for the fun of it. Those questions you asked! Nothing about schools, nothing about jobs, and you didn't even ask me what party I vote for. What kind of research is that? First, how many times a week you sleep with your husband, and then, do you find him handsome? It's total nonsense!'

Berna began to sweat again. Losing her concentration, she plucked a hair from the back of her neck. A cigarette, that was what she needed. *Oh, silly me.*

'But you see, our interest is in your motivations, we look at things from the psychological perspective.'

Ayşe was cold now. Her nostrils were flaring, and the veins in her forehead were beginning to bulge. *You think you can fool me, you liar?*

'The hell with your psychology!'

'I do beg your pardon... why are you being so aggressive? I assure you I won't bother you again!'

'You'd better not. And don't bother anyone else, either. No one's going to tell you the truth!'

Berna let her dressing gown fall from her shoulders, as she fingered the gold chain around her neck. For a moment she looked at the phone as if it were part of her own body. What did she have left to lose, and if something new came out of it...?

'You mean you didn't answer my questions truthfully?'

Ayşe let out a sour giggle. She sounded on the verge of tears.

'This husband of mine, for the past four years, he's been with another woman. And me? I'm no longer a woman, I'm all dried up inside, I'm all washed up. There isn't a hoca[14] I haven't been to see. Not a gynaecologist I haven't seen either. I have no tears left to cry, and at my age. I'm still so young! My breasts are *pert*! People think I'm a virgin and recommend me to their sons. Of course I lied! What was I going to say – that I let my husband go off with a prostitute?'

Berna got up from the bed to pace the room. The noise of the street was seeping into the shabby, smoke-filled apartment. Unknown ghosts swirled around her, and known ghosts, too. And once again, she felt herself one of them.

'Are you sure?'

'I'm sure! I rang all the numbers on his mobile, and I cursed every woman who answered. I went to the place where he works, and I looked each and every one of them up and down, asking myself who it was, and I cried, right in front of them, I picked fights, I disgraced myself. . .'

'Do you know who it is?'

'No trace of the bitch. No trace at all. I don't have that bitch's money, but it's clear to me that he's sexually smitten.'

'You mean he's in love with her?'

'Madly in love. When he falls in love, he turns into an animal, this husband of mine. His claws come out, and his eyes get bigger, and his shoulders rise like mountains. During those first years, there wasn't a part of me he didn't kiss. He wasn't coy, and he wasn't coarse. He would gaze straight into the light of my eyes, and find the most beautiful words to say to me. And he's doing the same to her now. He's making love to her like that now. Just like I taught him. If a man's been with one woman, it goes better with the next. And if I ever find that woman, I'll take her aside for a word or two.'

Berna fell back into bed. The fear in her voice had given way to compassion.

'What kind of woman do you think she is, then? Don't you ever wonder?'

'For years now, she's been in my dreams. One day I see

---

14. Teacher.

her as blonde, and the next day she's a brunette. She's plump, and flirtatious. If she had more brains than I do...'

'If she did...?'

'She'd come looking for me. If a woman's in love, she's not just going to sit there, she'll use her brains a little, she'll want to know about the woman she's sharing with. What would stop her? She'd play any trick...'

Ayşe heard a click, followed by a long, exasperating dial tone. Staring blankly at the receiver, she snapped, 'Hello? Are you there?' Joy radiated through her, as she straightened her back. She sucked in her stomach. She put down the receiver as gently as if she were putting it to sleep. She went into her bedroom and took a cardboard box out of a drawer, and inside she found the lipstick left over from the wedding. It was all dried up, but still she smiled.

# Yellow

TO MAKE UP FOR not having yet paid my respects to the grieving family, but also, just a little, fearing the smell of death, and never pausing to think if the gesture might cause offence, I bought an armful of roses. I had no idea how Nazan had felt about flowers. What I wanted (I think) was to breathe in the fragrance of roses while I was there. Not to honour her memory – these were just for me. I had been one of the first to hear of her death, but now a month had passed, and so – should my disrespect be met with sour looks – I would at least have an armful of roses, soothing me with their scent.

When I saw Seda Hanım, in a brown dress buttoned up to her throat, she looked better than I expected, I must say. And if she wore the expression of someone strangling herself with her own hands (she was, in any event, a woman who had long ago put her hopes out to dry) I wouldn't have expected anything else from her. Even so, there was a little curve in her lips, a secret smile as she opened the door, and a secret light in those red eyes. But when she saw me and my roses, she frowned and again took refuge behind the bruised veil of mourning. Her tears were not yet dry, and it wasn't immediately clear if she was still struggling to accept Nazan's absence. Ashamed to have subjected a member of the deceased's family to such a merciless inspection, I stepped inside and offered her my flowers. Accepting them with hesitation, Seda Hanım welcomed me into the house.

'I kept telling myself that you'd come by one of these days. I know how busy you are, so I wasn't at all offended. But these yellow roses – goodness. What can I say?'

Had I pleased her or upset her? I couldn't tell. Was I making light of her loss? Acting as if Nazan was still sick in bed, and not gone forever? I couldn't bear to dwell on such questions, and so I overdid it – threw my arms around her as if I were the cousin of the aunt of someone's uncle.

'I'm so sorry for your loss, Seda Hanım. Nazan was so young, it's such a shame.'

Extracting herself from my earnest embrace, she took the roses and set them gently on the sitting-room table. Instead of offering me a chair, she waved her thin arms in the direction of the stairs and led me up to Nazan's room on the top floor. I was thrown off balance by the harmony of colours in this house, which towered over its dusty neighbourhood, proud as a weeping fig. My connection to Nazan was a white engagement dress in French lace, embroidered with pearls the colour of bones. But here, in this house, Nazan's fine tailoring had given way to traditional furniture and contemporary art objects, to create a warm and personal space. I'd never noticed such discernment, or such stillness, in Seda Hanım or Nazan. Granted, I had just been a customer in search of a dress, but the thing is, whoever you're looking at, you should be able to have some small sense of the place where they live. Looking at these two, I had never imagined such a house. You needed courage to have walls the colour of dark smoke, and columns of contrasting red, and hand-painted borders, and those perfectly positioned giant wood-framed mirrors. The only thing wrong about this house was the presentiment of the great wrong that might result from moving just one thing out of place. No new object could be added; no object, however small, removed. Those yellow roses, lying downstairs on that table – I could see now that there was nowhere for them to go.

Entering Nazan's room, I felt a small chill pass through me, as an autumn breeze sailed through the small gap in the window to ruffle the lace curtain. It was upsetting, being made to sit on the bed of a dead woman, in this room done-up in white and emerald green. I was only here by force of custom – what sort of welcome was this? Seating herself on the handcrafted, round-armed chair next to the bed, Seda Hanım took a deep breath. How I longed to get up and go right then, but I couldn't move a muscle. As she spoke, she let her hand travel over the bedspread.

'She wasted away before our very eyes, the poor woman. She wasn't even 40. Not a single white hair. When she divorced Edip, they all came courting – general managers, bankers, high-ranking bureaucrats – but she turned them all away. Auntie, she said, let me live my life a little, but she never had a chance, and now she's gone. What were we to do? No one even knew what was ailing her.'

It was clear now that there was going to be no tea service, and that I ought not ask any questions. But then I made the mistake of glancing at the photographs on the walnut dresser, locked inside variously sized frames.

'We took that picture the day we opened our atelier for business. No money to speak of, but oh, how hard she worked to get it off the ground, with only her two hands to help her, and just one machine, working from morning until night, never stopping to eat or drink. Sometimes she couldn't even find time to wash her hair. Turning up cuffs, replacing zippers, making skirts overnight for teachers and officers' wives. Every bit of drudgery a seamstress might be called upon to do, she did. Before the year was out, she had her own boutique. She was ambitious, very ambitious. She changed our lives. All our lives.'

When I looked at the Nazan in the photograph – standing proudly, hiding her fatigue, her grey-blue eyes looking straight into me, as if she could read the future – I felt myself go hot all over. With those lace curtains fluttering in the window, all we needed was the score from *Wuthering Heights*. There she was, in the middle of the frame, her left leg crossed over her right leg, as if to clamp it into place, looking straight at me, in anger, as if she were about to ask me what I thought I was doing, sitting on her bed. I didn't know what

I was doing there either, or why Seda Hanım had chosen to wear such a disagreeable dress today, or why she was so eager to prattle on like this, and show me these photographs, and open all these drawers for me. My plan had been to give her the roses and go.

'In that big black and white photo, it's me and my elder sister – Nazan's mother – and Nazan. Even when she was young, you could tell she was going to be a beauty like her mother. They say girls get their fate from their mothers. How strange that they both died around the age of 40, though of course in her mother's case, it wasn't an illness. Who would have thoughtthat such a joyous woman would hang herself one day… Well, maybe it was being orphaned that made Nazan resilient, because whatever she set her mind to, she did. When my sister died, I said to Nazan, if you like, you can call me mother, but she never did. I was always just her silly Aunt Seda. Do you know, when the boutique started doing well, she offered to pay me a salary? I'd actually put a great deal of work in, to get that boutique off the ground, so it hurt me, hurt me terribly in fact, to be offered a salary, as if I were just one of the girls. I mean, I accepted it, but the insult never stopped smarting.' Seda Hanım had no sooner uttered these words than the pendulum of death swung back across her pale face. And in her half-smile I read guilt – and relief. 'Well I suppose that's how you become successful over the years, how you become society's favourite seamstress – didn't she sew you an engagement dress, too?'

Still playing the listener, I nodded. It seemed to be dawning on Seda Hanım that I was not particularly keen to hear every last detail of Nazan's story, and she clasped her freckled hands now, as though she was about to conjure an amusing sentence in conclusion, but then her fingers went to the buttons on her dress collar.

'Did you know that this dress I'm wearing is the last one Nazan ever sewed? Actually, I'd have preferred something in honey yellow, but she insisted it had to be brown. Silly, really, but for years I never noticed Nazan's aversion to yellow. If customers came with golden fabric, or yellow taffeta, she'd just say that she had too much work on, and with that she'd turn her back, and I could never understand it, given how much our Nazan liked money. If anyone asked for something yellow, she'd say, this other colour would suit you better, and change the customer's mind. Funny – I brought the poor girl up myself and somehow never noticed. Her brother – Bahadır, I mean – he understood everything much better than I did.'

She opened up a drawer in the white chest that stood between us and took out a photograph of a young man. She made to smooth out its bent corners. A graduation portrait, a young man in his mortar-board cap. But in his eyes – such malevolence! So at odds with the magnificent elation of youth. No, this was a private gaze, never to be put on proud display. No one had ever kissed those cheeks goodnight. Or those thin, girlish eyebrows, those clenched, sour, angry lips.

'Nazan never left him wanting, not for a single day. Whatever his friends had, he had too, and when he started university, she even bought him a car. She could be a bit stern with him, a bit domineering, but he never raised his voice at her. And, God bless, he became a most capable interior designer. He'd restore houses for Nazan's society customers, and soon he was making good money, even more than Nazan. They actually pooled their money to buy this house.'

I struggled to imagine how a young man could bear living in a house like this, this mausoleum to all the colours in the palette but one. All that remained of the sad story, a story in which Seda Hanım herself seemed to play no part, was a big house that would admit no yellow. But it had been the thin-armed Seda Hanım who had opened the curtains with such childish surprise, as if to summon a great actor, and shown me Nazan's room.

'You can see Bahadır's eye everywhere in this house, but it was on this room that he lavished the most care. Floral patterns we couldn't even name, hand-made glass *objets d'arts*, Italian fittings we'd only seen in magazines… Overnight Bahadır turned our lives into a dream. Of course he never used yellow. That's why I was so shocked when I saw those yellow roses in your arms. I hope they haven't dried out. You're the first one who's ever brought yellow into this house. To get this emerald green hue on these walls? I cannot begin to tell you how many different colours he had to mix, and do you see the border? Bahadır drew that pattern by hand. Day and night, he searched for the right designs…'

When I inspected the fine lines of the border's floral pattern, I hardly had the will to appreciate the force with which Bahadır had tamed those mutinous waves. It was a flower that had never opened its petals anywhere in the world, and this most beautiful design had been his gift to his sister. I looked at that flower, and looked, and looked…

'But as soon as Nazan moved in here, she fell ill. "I feel so troubled when I sleep in here," she said. Perhaps we shouldn't have indulged her.'

It had orange leaves, webbed with green. A flower that reminded me of a clover…

'Before, she was always the one who woke at the crack of dawn, to open up the shop. She didn't like rising in sunlight. But now she couldn't even get out of bed, started sleeping until noon, and wouldn't eat a thing. From one day to the next, she faded away, and such laziness, such sloth, she wouldn't even comb her hair, or put on make-up. She really let herself go, poor thing. We thought it was cancer. No stone was left unturned. Check-ups, MRIs, anti-depressants, nothing did any good.'

Sprouting from the centre were stamens – like purple sex organs – spilling out in all directions, almost shouting.

'Bahadır never left his sister's side; he gave up work to look after her. He held her hand, caressed her hair, and when I think of how he was at the end, I feel a fever coming on. It'd been years since I'd seen those two so close.'

I looked at Bahadır's flower. I looked and I looked. I looked at its sidelong curve, at the raw grey drops decorating the border's edge.

I jumped to my feet, saying I had things to do. As I left that great house where colour had taken its revenge, as I climbed to the top of that vexing hill, I vowed not to breathe a word about what I had seen. On those impossible flowers, on the tips of those purple stamens, I had seen the faintest hint of yellow, but I did not, could not, tell a soul.

# Tacettin

So THERE HE WAS, our Tidy Tacettin, but totally wasted, a wreck on two legs, and when they saw him coming down the street, swaying like a camel, pissed out of his mind, they closed in on him and tried to steal his wallet. No way our man could know who these idiots were. Beardless, tightass Beyoğlu boys, fresh out of Adana! Cowards, every one, or why would they wait until the middle of the night to pick on a drunk? If you saw Tacettin you'd put him at five foot five inches more or less. Built like a tree trunk. A really thick one, too. With a neck twice the size of yours and maybe five times the size of mine. The great one in the sky had something special in mind for Tacettin – when He reached down to the earth he used all his might to press down on our man's head until He had squashed it like Erzurum cheese. Tacettin's fingers were like millstones – put a few grains of corn between them and, abracadabra, you had corn flour. He might not be so tall, our man, but he was wide as a tree, and if you saw his hands, with all those hairs sprouting from his fingers, you'd think you were looking at bear claws. I saw him once at the hamam[15] – if the man didn't shave, you'd think they were letting in gorillas.

So now Tacettin is drunk, and stinking of rakı, but that doesn't stop him. His arms have lives of their own, you know. One second they're folded. Next second they're striking like snakes. He has one of those beardless youths by the throat

---

15. A traditional bath house.

now, and the boy is gasping, blubbering, bleating like a sheep. So now Tacettin raises his arm. Then he lifts the boy higher, and Mr Beardless starts going purple. As far as I know, Tacettin has never taken a life with his own hands – he never sets out to kill people. Just to scare them. He could be a killer, but intimidation, that's his art, and he's a master. The other boy is the bleating lamb's brother, believe it or not, and then he starts yelling like the neighbourhood whore. So now the hyenas of the backstreets come piling in to kick Tacettin's wretched balls and retune his ribs. And what do you know, but the bleating lamb turns into a lion suddenly – you know how some dogs don't bark until they've joined the pack, well it turns out this boy is one of them. He takes out a knife and cuts right into Tacettin's cheek. They're thicker than leather, but this boy cuts so deep he hits a vein. And then those cut-rate grave robbers go to work. They take his watch, his ring, his wallet, everything. Meanwhile Tacettin is clocking them with his little black X-ray eyes so that when the time is right, he'll know who to go after (although in truth, it's ten against one, and he doesn't have eyes in the back of his head, so it could be anyone). Now Tacettin's broken rib is cutting into his liver, and the less said about his face, the better. After staggering around for a while, he drops to the ground and passes out.

Then there are these two policemen, sitting in the shadows in their car. That's what they all do – they just sit in their cars and wait. Leave those street crowds to do their own dirty work, they say. 'Let dog eat dog,' they say, and they keep on saying it until their arses are as wide as mountain pastures. It's four o'clock in the morning now, and the whole place is salty with blood, when finally they wander over to take a look. Tacettin's eye has almost slid down one cheek, and there's that deep gash in the other cheek. The blood is pouring out. One of the policemen is this great big fatso, with a belly so large it's grazing against his knees, while the other is a greenhorn; no one's scraped his bonnet yet, or splattered his shoes with blood. When he sees the shape Tacettin's in, he just stands there, arms hanging, like an idiot. Come on now, you fool, you waited long enough already, so now do something – throw him into the back of your car, why don't you? Get him to Taksim Emergency! But oh no, these two just stand over Tacettin like rainclouds – totally still, like they're on a film set. Forget emergencies, they have a report to write.

The young one's conscience is bothering him, though. He's too new to be callous (but let's see him in two years – by then even his tear ducts will have shrivelled up). He turns to the older one and says we should have got here sooner, and while he's still muttering like the coward he is, he grabs Tacettin by the neck and then the waist and tries to pull him up. Fatso follows on, doing what he can. Now, Tacettin must weigh as much as three bags of cement, so when he's finally on Mr Handsome's back, the cop is swaying like a keychain as he swaggers towards the car. They throw him into the back seat, push in his legs, and at long last, they speed off. And perhaps if Tacettin had woken up right then, things would have worked out a little different.

When he does come to, he's in a room reeking of medicine, with fluorescent lights shining right into his eyes, and next to him is this giggling idiot of a nurse. What's she laughing at? What else but Tacettin's feet. Tacettin always wore size seven shoes, you see, but that night we found out that he had feet as small as a woman's, and it seems our friend was pretty embarrassed about that, so embarrassed that he was in the habit of stuffing a pair of those fancy ladies' shoulder pads behind his ankles. So this girl is there with the shoulder pads in her hands, showing the orderlies how small his feet are, and just think about it – we have a man here with a 45-inch-waist, and shoulders like boulders, and arms that can spread wider than an eagle – all this, with a pair of girl's feet. Now who wouldn't find that funny?

When Tacettin clocks that the girl is laughing at him, he gives her a good kick. When the girl's smirk turns into a whinnying whine, something you'd expect from a mosquito, this curly-haired doctor who looks like Michaelangelo's David steps inside. He's about to give the patient what for, but no. One look at Tacettin there in bed and the situation changes. He pushes the girl away and asks for another nurse. And in comes this kakanoz,[16] and I'm not using the word lightly. This nurse has to be one of the most hideous creatures on the planet. She's seen it all, this kakanoz. And you know how it is − sometimes, when there's a job to be done, you need people like that around. They take one look, and measure it up against the years. So anyway, this kakanoz takes one long frowning look at Tacettin's split cheek and gets out her tools and starts cleaning him up. But now Doctor David has to say his piece. And when Tacettin hears him saying this is a judicial matter, call the hospital police, he sits right up. The man has spent two hours on the ground unconscious, bleeding on all sides, with two of his own ribs digging into him like knives, but now we see that pain does Tacettin good − it sharpens his wits, helps with his recovery, even. You could even say it turns him on. I don't want any police, he says. Sew this up and I'll get the fuck out. But David of the Curly Hair is a soldier and he's determined to do his duty. His left eye starts twitching, as if to say, we're not in one of your gambling dens now. This happens to be a hospital. He throws the nurse a glance and, shlickshlack, he slips on his rubber gloves.

I don't know what this hideous nurse's name is. Let's call her Necla; we don't want to be unkind to the old girl. There's a little grey in her hair, and three crow's feet at the edge of each eye. She's seen better days, in other words. Her eyes are as cold as an owl's. So not your typical Necla, Necla being a name that makes you think of poetry and song. It travels on a puff of air, on a sigh. *Ah, Necla…* Like that.

Time to sew up that wound, but by now Tacettin's face has swollen up like a loaf of bread, and the guy's ears are

---

16. An ugly person.

ringing. Before anyone can say let's give this man a sedative, dear God, we have visitors. It's the chief of the hospital's Incident Investigation Police. A hairless, bloodless, yellow-skinned, gnat-faced, pig's ass named Selahattin. He walks over to Tacettin on his little bow legs, this Selahattin, and in his shrill little voice, he says, who did this to you, brother? After this, a long silence. Necla is cleaning the dried blood off Tacettin's nose by now, and when Tacettin hears that voice, he begins to turn that thick head of his, oh so slowly, slow as a ship's wheel, and when he sees the shadow of a man in a police uniform, he jumps up, roaring. Didn't I say no police, you idiots? he bellows. He takes tiny Selahattin by his shoulders and shakes him, shakes him hard, and then he takes that stone he calls his forehead, and butts Selahattin in the nose. The orderly clears the room, with Selahattin still lying there on the floor, while Necla glares at Tacettin with her little black eyes, and as for Dr David, well, he doesn't look so sure of himself now; he's quaking like my grandmother sifting flour. Tacettin goes snarling back to bed, to lie down for Necla, while two men come in to attend to Selahattin, who's still unconscious. David's sorry arse is clenched, and he's standing well back. Necla looks down at the policeman. She threads her needle and gives it to the doctor. The crowd at the door is gone by now – all those nosey pickle-makers have fled.

Dr David's syringe misses the vein somehow, so forget about sedatives, forget about waiting for the anaesthetic to take effect. He begins to sew up Tacettin's cheek like it was a quilt. I say sew, but there's no sign of skill or care. I could have done it better myself. You'd have thought that pimp was sewing a ripped pair of trousers. Who could care less about Tacettin's face? But now the word's gone out to the force that some hoodlum they brought into casualty smashed Selahattin's nose. So let's take a look at this monster they all say, and they pile into casualty. They wrap their hands around their flashy truncheons, and they jiggle them quietly, to send Tacettin a message. Tacettin turns around, and he sees the filth, four policemen, all six-footers, special forces. So now Tacettin pushes Dr David aside. He jumps to his feet, and his face begins to bleed again. Tacettin has a thing about police, you see. He can't bear the sight of them. He bellows, 'Didn't I tell you idiots to stay away?' And then he lets out a string of curses, and lays into them. The five of them spill into the corridor in a tangled knot, where other patients, who happen to be waiting outside, line up along the walls like bags of refuse. Tacettin butts one policeman in the head, lands his fist on another… Whoever comes near him, the man's playing a bone solo. No one's stupid enough to try and break them up, so they just stand there, gawping. A few of the women begin screaming so loud you'd think the truncheons were landing on their own backs. And so it goes on, for five or ten minutes – they beat each other up. They beat Tacettin up good, and the Gestapo also gets its due. They all have busted lips and eyebrows, and one's been kicked in the stomach and is now doubled over in pain. You can no more hold Tacettin back than a sex-crazed dog. And when their mouths go dry and their ears get ripped, the police eventually back off a bit, so the two orderlies see their chance and drag Tacettin back into his room. The only one left in there is Necla. She's still in that room, waiting with her instruments. David of the Curly Hair is long gone. Once again, Tacettin shakes off the two orderlies clinging to his arms, and he falls against Necla's shoulder. So much blood on his face now that you can't even see it. So our dear Necla starts to clean him up, saying nothing. There are now five gashes on Tacettin's face. He has a busted eyebrow, a busted lip, and a broken nose.

Clenching his fist, he looks up at Necla, and he yells, 'You tell them that if they send any more police in here, next time will be even worse!' No curses, though. He's talking to a woman.

Necla gives Tacettin a long look – she's sitting there with bandages in her hand. 'That's fine, my brother. Don't worry. The police aren't coming back.'

And Tacettin falls back into bed like a lump of dough, while Necla anesthetizes his face, and then, very slowly, begins to sew. Nothing tidy about Tacettin now, his shirt ripped, his chest bared, everything in tatters. He lifts his arm and begins to cry. But what a sound he makes! This guy is bawling. Blubbering! And Necla, she's never heard anything like it. The man is braying like a donkey. Now that's what I call daring. If any zamazingo[17] got wind of Tacettin crying, he'd never hear the end of it. What people don't understand, though, is that when a man has been beaten and shredded, there's nothing left to do but cry. But you've got to make sure you're with the right person, and the one person Tacettin can trust in this fickle world is Necla. Not a muscle moves on that face of hers. If you could see her sitting there, you'd think she was listening to the evening news. She just sits while Tacettin cries. She doesn't even look at his face. And then, in that low voice of hers, low as the thickest string of a violin, she says, I told you not to worry, the police aren't coming back. Tacettin gives the woman's hand a squeeze. That's all. He's not bothered. He doesn't even look at Necla's face. He just closes his eyes and drifts off to sleep like a little boy.

These days he drops by the Taksim Emergency at least once a month, to look in on Necla. If you ask him why, well, while staring into her eyes, Tacettin got a rub of the magic lamp. She's special, you see. She's the only one in this fickle world who has ever seen Tidy Tacettin cry.

---

17. Old Istanbul slang for 'riff-raff'.

# Army Story

As HE LEFT THE university hospital's forensic medicine building and made for the garden – where some visitors waited on benches, their heads buried in their hands, and others were pacing anxiously back and forth – the colonel was already unsteady on his feet. His face was the colour of lime. It was all he could do to hold up his head as he staggered about; a dark green lump in search of a place to sit. He took off his cap and put it under his arm. He was still looking for a seat, but the benches were all full of patients' friends and relatives. He had no choice but to sink down onto one of the concrete slabs bordering the flowerbeds, not far from a young woman. As he wiped his forehead with his handkerchief, he tried to hide his tears. It was August 1987, and when this colonel, collapsed by the flowerbeds, undid the buttons on his collar and began to laugh, and sway with morbid wails, the crowded scene around the university hospital grew more piteous still.

The young woman who was sitting close by fetched a bottle of water from her plastic bag and took it over to him.

'Here, have some water.'

The colonel took the bottle and twisted off the cap. He poured some water into the palm of his hand and splashed it over his forehead.

'Thank you,' he said, 'the heat was really getting to me.'

'Is your relative going to be all right? Or are they in intensive care?'

The colonel tensed up. Rising from the ground, he buttoned up his collar. His eyes were bloodshot.

'It's not my relative. It's my soldier. He's dead. The boy's dead.'

Concerned now, the girl came closer still. 'I'm so sorry for your loss. What happened? A skirmish?'

'They found him dead in his bed. They're still investigating, to find out why. Thank you for the water.' The colonel started walking away. The girl was more or less talking to herself by now.

'May God protect those left behind. May He set the poor creature free at once. Let him be buried now, and find peace.'

The colonel stopped. He was having trouble walking. When he staggered to one side, the girl jumped up to steady him by the arm.

'Are you all right? You need to be careful.'

'My head was spinning.'

'You have a difficult job, being responsible for so many young men. May God ease your way.'

The colonel turned towards the woman and began to speak, splattering her with spit.

'I went to see the doctor in forensics just now. They'd cut the boy up. For two days now, they've been cutting him up. Today I went in there, and there was no head. And I lost my temper. They have no respect, these brutes. They'd tossed it somewhere, rolled it onto another gurney. A doctor the same age as you took it by the hair, carried it over, and left it next to his body. Next to his buttocks.'

Horrified, the young woman cried, 'But that's a sin! A very great sin!'

The colonel was having a hard time speaking. His words were burning his tongue. 'When I saw that head like that, sitting next to his buttocks… that child… Well, at least this made him look a bit more like a human being.'

As the colonel moved away, cap in hand, and struggling to keep his balance, the door of the military jeep parked in the distance flew open. The adjutant stood waiting, holding his salute, straight as a nail.

The previous day, during Ordnance Senior Colonel Nedim Zeybek's meeting with Senior Consultant Yücel Kavaklı in a consultation room in the Forensic Medicine Department of Ninth September University, the lifeless body of Private Uğur Ergönen, Martyr, was lying stretched out on the gurney. There was a deep incision stretching from his lung cavity to his abdomen. Enervated by the odour of medicine, and also by the flat sheen of the room's chrome instruments, Colonel Nedim soon lost his patience.

'Don't bombard me with medical terminology! Best if I ask the questions and you give the answers.'

During his years of service, the doctor had grown accustomed to the imperious ways of state officials, so now he joined his hands behind his back and said. 'Yes, Colonel, let's do as you suggest.'

'Did this child commit suicide?'

'There is no evidence that he did. Look, there are no marks on his neck. Nowhere on his body have we found any cuts, bruises or abrasions. He did not fall, and nothing was crushed. If pressure had been put on his chest, we'd have found contusions in his lungs, and breaks in his lobes.

The colonel glanced quickly at the soldier's lungs. 'So you mean to say that the lungs are in good condition?'

'Yes. There's no sign of pressure, or crushing.'

'Could he have taken an overdose?'

'We've run all the tests, and the lab found no sign of sleeping pills or other chemicals.'

'So you're saying that the boy just hiccupped and died.'

'I just don't know. In the beginning I suspected a traumatic arterial spasm. This happens now and again with multiple bone fractures. Fractures can cause contusions and corrosions in the arteries; there's not necessarily a lesion on the skin.'

'Let's keep to the point. Were there or weren't there broken bones?'

'No, colonel, we found no broken bones.'

'Maybe they smothered him. There are a number of maniacs in that barracks.'

'No one smothered him. There was some sign of pressure on his lungs, but no bleeding. And there's no sign of hands having put pressure on him, or pillows.'

'At the end of the day, this boy died for a reason!'

'Of course he did, of course. Tomorrow we are going to examine the brain. While there's no sign that he fell, no crack in his skull, it's possible he died from internal epidural bleeding. Or meningitis. That's another possibility. The last thing I can suggest is fat embolism syndrome. But it tends to target the lungs. Macroglobulin fats –'

'That's enough, doctor. Find out what killed him so that I can write the report. We can't say that he just dropped dead.'

'His liver, spleen, and kidneys were slightly enlarged. There could be an issue with his circulatory system. In a short while we're taking his heart out, to see if there's any sign of an infarction. It's only a small possibility, but –'

'Do you suspect a heart attack?'

'Not really, but we'll look into it, of course.'

'You could have looked at the child's heart before cutting him all up like this.'

'As I said earlier, colonel, my first suspicion was battery.'

'I want the report at the earliest opportunity. You send it to me first, before it goes to the military prosecutor, do you hear?'

'As you wish.'

As soon as the colonel left the consultation room, he spat on the floor. He could still taste that air, sticking to his tongue.

On 14<sup>th</sup> August 1987 – the day before his lifeless body was sent off for autopsy – Private Uğur Ergören did not turn up for morning roll call. Specialist Sinan Sarı, who was in charge of the barracks, and found the solider dead in his cot, reported that his chin was sagging and his tongue protruding slightly. His friends, who had known Uğur as the boy from Hatay, refused to leave his side until the army medic had arrived. They put ice on his body, to help preserve him in the hellish heat. As they were carrying out the soldier, covered from head to toe, everyone inside the barracks began to wail. Some of these soldiers were crying, and others grieved with curses.

Two days before Private Uğur's death, Colonel Nedim went into the adjutant's office at around 4am to find him dozing while on night duty, his head on his desk. He hovered anxiously over the boy, who had his nose buried inside his cap. He had only come in from basic training a few weeks earlier, and he still hadn't learned to jump to his feet when still asleep. For a while, Colonel Nedim just stood there, watching. Then he leaned over and gently tugged the boy's ear. Uğur jumped to his feet in fear, immediately standing to attention.

'Yes, sir!'

'It was the first time he had seen the colonel in an undershirt and combat trousers. In a voice gentle as well as stern, the colonel said, 'You mustn't fall asleep, my child. Even if your officer falls asleep, you must keep your eyes open.'

'Yes, sir!'

'You don't need to shout so loud. And now you can go and make me a coffee, no sugar.'

'At once, sir.'

Returning to the colonel's room with the coffee, Uğur did not take his eyes off that cup. Now Colonel Nedim was bare to his waist, leafing through a magazine in the light of the table lamp. The air from ventilator in the corner was making some pages turn by themselves. There was a silly, and slightly menacing, smile on Colonel Nedim's face.

Putting the cup on the table, Uğur saluted again. 'Do you have another order for me, sir?' He was standing so straight that his adam's apple looked like it was about to fly from his throat.

'At ease, soldier.'

Uğur put his hands behind his back.

'It's very hot, isn't it?'

'Yes, sir, it's very hot.'

'Antakya's even hotter right now.'

'Yes, sir, it's even hotter there.'

'Where do you people sleep in those parts nowadays? On the roof?'

'I used to sleep on the balcony, sir.'

'To catch those lovely breezes. Why not just say so? While here we bathe in our own sweat.'

The colonel took one more sip of his coffee before standing up. His stomach was sagging over his trousers. Stepping in front of Uğur, he gazed for a few moments at his face.

'How old are you?'

'Twenty years old, sir!'

'Everyone else is trying to get out of their military service, but here you are. You have no family, I hear.'

'No, sir, I grew up in an orphanage.'

'Do you have any idea who your parents were?'

'My mother died when I was little, and then my father left me at the orphanage.'

Uğur watched the colonel pacing madly back and forth in the lamp's harsh light. As the colonel spoke, he kept his eyes on the ground. 'Did you ever hear from your father again?'

'I was told he worked in Tuzla and died a few years after he left me.'

'Don't you have any family at all – an uncle, or an aunt?'

'No, sir. I have no one.'

'It must have been hard for you, growing up alone, in the orphanage and so on. Speak, my son. Relax.'

'Yes, sir, it was hard. But now it's behind me, thank goodness.'

'You're an electrician, aren't you?'

'Yes, sir. I'm a vocational school graduate.'

'You have your own shop, don't you?'

'I hope to open one as soon as I get back, sir.'

Colonel Nedim was fingering his lips. Smiling, he turned back to Uğur. 'You're a beautiful boy, a very handsome fellow indeed. I'll bet those Antakya girls follow you everywhere.'

For the first time, Uğur relaxed enough to nod. He was ashamed to have smiled. Just then the colonel cupped his hands around Uğur's face and pulled him close. Feeling the colonel's wet lips on his face, Uğur pushed him back with all his strength.

'What you are doing, you brute.'

Falling back onto the desk, Colonel Nedim knocked over the lamp. A small crash and the colonel's room was plunged into darkness. The smell of spilt coffee grew steadily stronger. Uğur opened the door to make his escape. In the naked light of the side room, the colonel was now a stiff shadow. Hissing between his teeth, he said, 'Step out of this room and I'll fuck your grandmother.'

Uğur stopped. The colonel was pointing his gun at him. At a loss, he just stood there.

'For the love of God, let me go…'

'I'll say you pounced on me in the dead of night,' said the colonel. 'I'll say there was a struggle. I'll say I had no choice but to defend myself. I'll shoot you between the eyes!'

Crying, and biting his fist, Uğur yelled, 'God damn you, you shameless bastard!'

'Shut the door. Shut it now!'

Uğur shut the door and went back into the room. He felt so alone in the dark. All he could hear was the whine of the ventilator and the colonel's heavy breathing. Before long, he felt the barrel of a gun pressing against his chin. And then the colonel's coffee-scented lips. After the colonel had caressed his shoulders, he took Uğur's penis in his hand and pumped it hard. He began to mumble, his voice thick with lust.

'How many days, boy, how many days now that I haven't stopped thinking about you? All those sidelong glances. All that licking of lips. Those little ironic smiles when you bring me my coffee. You've been toying with me for days.'

In a trembling voice, Uğur pleaded with Colonel Nedim, whom he could barely see. 'But I'm not a queer, sir. If I'm lying, God strike me dead. But I'm not a queer.'

Still holding his gun, the colonel pulled Uğur towards him.

'So do some people call you a queer, my little lion? You're hung like a steed, God bless. Come closer, let me see…'

As Colonel Nedim opened Uğur's cartridge belt, Uğur tried and failed to fend him off. 'But sir, I'm engaged.'

'Good, so when you get married you can tell your wife. It will be one of your army stories.'

# Nine Sons

31 DECEMBER 2000
To: The Principal Clerk,
Ministry of Agriculture and Rural Areas

Please find attached a petition that was sent to us from Adana. Having established that it is not within our remit, we are forwarding it to you. The petition contains a denunciation with regard to the illegal manufacture of alcohol (rakı). We would be grateful if you could inform the Interior Ministry after taking the necessary measures.

    Kindly submitting our respects,
General Secretary
Ministry of the Environment
*Petition attached*

22 January 2001
To: The General Secretary,
Ministry of Public Works and Settlements

We would like to direct your attention to a petition from one of our citizens about the flood disaster in Erzurum. The works in the disaster area are the statutory responsibility of your ministry.

    With my respects,
The Principal Clerk
Ministry of Agriculture and Rural Areas
*Petition attached*

14 February 2001
To: The Commission on Health, Family, Labour, and Social Affairs

We are in receipt of a complaint in relation to an on-going blood feud in the village of Halfeti, in the district of Erzurum.
We are sending it on to you for your information, passing on our respects.
General Secretary,
Ministry of Public Works and Settlements
*Petition attached.*


4 April 2001
To: The Ministry of Defence

We are in receipt of a petition sent to us from Germany concerning a guest worker currently working abroad, with regard to his military service. We are sending it to you for your inspection, and with our respects,
The Commission on Health, Family, Labour, and Social Affairs
*Petition attached.*


17 June 2001
To the Prime Ministry of the Turkish Republic

Please find attached a request that falls outside our remit. We are forwarding this petition, which is addressed to the Prime Minister, with our best wishes and respects. The petition is concerned with local problems connected to the election of a village muhtar.
The General Secretariat,
Ministry of Defence
*Petition attached.*

TO: THE PRIME MINISTER OF THE TURKISH
REPUBLIC
ANKARA
16 December 2000

Dear Prime Minister,

With so many petitions passing across your desk, I have no
way of knowing if mine will catch your eye. All right then,
but if you do happen to be reading these clumsily written
words, you will hear the strong, greying, tearful voice of man
who served for seven years as the muhtar of Halfeti, only to
be cut off from the winding cliffs of the Euphrates. This is a
voice that sang a thousand folksongs before reaching
manhood, that herded cattle in the dust of spring, that came
to love pistachio trees at the age of nine, that at ten climbed
down into the Rumkale well to drink its first oath, that at 14
was fairly smothered by bathtub rakı, and at 18 found its way
into its sweetheart's ear. If you can't hear it, then that's your
business, but here's what it has to say if you can: it's over. You
left it too late.

However many deputies you have in that lofty assembly
of yours, we opened our arms to each and every one. We gave
our full and undivided attention to more speeches than we
can count. People came, and people went, and our hands
swelled from all the clapping. For each and every one, we
sacrificed a sheep. Not a single slave of God amongst them
told us that our houses and homes were going to end up
underwater. We are simple villagers, and we know but one
patch of this earth. The blue sky is our atlas. When the sky
clouds over, we know it's going to rain, and when the earth
turns red, we know it's spring. But we could not read the lies

in your deputies' dimples. *Aman,*[18] we said, let's see if our Prime Minister will take an interest.

Our nights were the deepest, loveliest blue, and our women the most adorned with flowers. Spread out before us: the Euphrates; above our heads: the stars. Our bellies were full, the sun was on our backs. We were the most industrious workers of the earth's reddest soil. We knew how to love the capricious pistachio tree for 25 long years, without ever showing our temper. I don't know if you ever happened to come and see our gardens. Our olive trees were the coyest. Winter and summer, they stayed green (the stone vats we used to extract the oil – they're growing moss now). And then there were the figs, babbling to themselves in the breeze, like fine gentlemen. They were most generous with what they had. Their leaves were as wide as trays, and when they lifted them to the sun, they gave us food, and not just us, but also the birds flying down from the sky. The fig is the kind of tree that can tower over a house like a father keeping watch on his children. You can't climb a fig tree, and you can't play backgammon in its shadow, but whatever it has, you can take. Oleasters are a breed apart, and so are mulberries, and cypresses, and pomegranate trees, and grapevines. If you'd wanted to know how green green was, and how yellow yellow, all you had to do was come and ask us. But you waited too long. And the pistachio trees. Yes, them. If you had seen the pistachio trees, well, a single glimpse and they'd have loosened your tongue. On winter nights, with their slender branches, they would open their arms like praying white imams as they wandered in our midst. Each with a long, straggling beard, and eyes the colour of night. Go ahead and say you don't believe me, but each and every pistachio tree possessed the power to rise from its roots and walk, as a dervish dede. Even the great Euphrates would ripple quietly along his path. He showed his majesty to the Euphrates, but it hid it from your engineers, and your politicians.

---

18. For goodness' sake.

As you know, there's a town near Halfeti called Nizip. Once upon a time there was a place there called 'Yellow Cave' and it was swarming with demons. Bandits would stop the caravans that passed by, and abduct the businessmen and tradesmen, and when they got to this cave, they would peel them like onions. When Mustafa Kemal[19] took charge of the nation, he got word that every time this cave squeezed its haunches, it gave birth to another bandit, and so he had a guard post stationed in front of it. After the guard post went up, not a single bandit remained in Nizip; they all went flying off to other parts, like fleas. They couldn't get near the cave until after the time of İsmet Paşa.[20] But by then, it was too late, Prime Minister. You know how I said those pistachio trees could walk. Well, Yellow Cave could walk like that, too. All the way to Ankara. What you need to understand is this: the cave now sits inside Ankara's own belly. It's there, right in front of you. Can't you see it?

And guess what: when you were plugging the winding Euphrates with your dam, turning it into a lake, this cave was at work. To submerge our lives, our homes, our manna – this land we tamed with our own hands – all this was the cave's idea. You cast us onto the wuthering rocks. Old ladies' knees are aching, and their hearts are sinking to their livers. However much they had to teach us – in sayings and in songs, on the saz[21] or in prayer, be advised – it's all fading into their breasts. Young men who know only of the soil stare stupidly at the rocks, and as for the women, they wear black, and they no longer laugh. The brides have no more milk, and their babes pull at plastic teats. Lovers exchanging desirous looks are parted by the waters. Should one of us die, we have no mosque to say prayers over him. Our old mosque is just sitting there like a post in the middle of the lake. You made a dam, but what a disaster. Let it be known that you made a terrible mistake.

---

19. Mustafa Kemal Atatürk (1891-1938), first president of Turkey.
20. Mustafa İsmet İnönü (1884-1973), second president of Turkey.
21. A long-necked lute, also known as a 'bağlama'.

The last thing I want to say is this, Prime Minister: one day soon I shall die. If you're thinking of coming to these parts, to ask after me – don't! They'll tell you I said a lot of things behind your back. He complained until the day he died, they'll say. But don't take offence! And be advised that I have nine sons to survive me. I sent them all to Germany. One is studying to be an engineer, another is gazing at the sky and counting stars. My middle son is courting a girl, and he sings her folksongs day and night. The biggest of the little ones is a lion of a wrestler; the littlest is even now writing out prescriptions for family and friends alike. Not a single one is left in these parts. You surrendered 5,000 hectares of red soil to the Euphrates, and I surrendered my nine sons. Let them stay where they are and never come back. If there's no land, there's no homeland. Know this too: if you're still thinking of coming here one day, saying, 'So where are these nine sons?', well, save yourself the trouble. Ali, Ferhat, Mustafa, Kemal, Celal, Cevahir, Hüseyin, Hasan, and Yusuf – they're all lost to you now.

Bring together all the men you can find, and you'll still be nine sons short. That's when you should pay a visit to Yellow Cave. They'll know exactly what to do with you.

Mehmet Kara
Halfeti the Nameless
L blok
No:28

# Deep Inside

AFTER THEY HAD FINISHED making love, the man got up to fetch a glass of water, and that was when the woman noticed how ugly his feet were. One glance and she was sitting bolt upright. Clutching her head – this head that had been silly enough to have found this man with these ugly feet attractive, even seductive – she subjected them to a closer examination. Hardened soles stretching out like planks, arches encased in cartilage. Thick vessels bursting with the body's filth. Layered toenails, thick and sharp enough to rip anything they touched. Yellowed, calloused toes. A jutting ankle bone. Skin as thick and brown as leather. Dear God! Are these the feet I've just slept with? Denied their share of human flesh, and the rush of mad love, they had bided their time, even during the desperate, undercover struggle to free themselves of socks, until they finally joined in, uninvited. Then they savoured each moment, each tremor of love, right down to the tips of those toes, having risen up against their master to claim their share, by contriving to brush against a soft little foot. And then, when it was all over, they'd slipped out to reveal themselves, feeling no shame, not even for the black hairs sprouting from every toe. Can these really be the feet I've just slept with?

She looked over at the man, now back in bed with her, a smile masking her thoughts. Taken in by her gaze, he planted a kiss on her cheek. After all, he had no idea that his feet seemed like aliens to her – he'd never even considered feet to be objects of aesthetic value – and now, as he lay in

143

this room thick with the musk of wild love, basking in this woman's impish, enticing smile, he wasn't going to second-guess her feelings. He had no idea his feet had turned her stomach. He got up again and paced the hotel room naked, taking deep drags from his cigarette, feeling just fine.

Parting the thick curtains that had given the room its dark aura of romance, the man stared out at the wooded hill across the way. How long he'd been planning this visit! How long he'd dreamed of falling back, all passion spent, onto a feather bed with the woman he'd loved for many months now! He had wanted to reach deep inside her, burrow into that ample pearly light and set it free, then be at one with the green hill he now saw before him. He recalled how patiently he'd waited for this moment when he could bring her to this secluded mountain hotel, and savour, with these hills, love's first caress. He gave his thigh a gentle scratch; it sounded more like crunching in the hushed room, which only moments ago had been awash with passion. Reliving those heights, he felt the sun's golden rays piercing his chest, while on the hill opposite, autumn had begun to paint the leaves red. He smiled out at them. It was all he could do not to whistle. Stubbing out his cigarette, he turned to the woman. 'Come on. Let's go out for a walk.'

She sniffled under the covers. The strings of her heart snapped one by one. She said, 'We'll only get cold. Let's not.'

'It's a beautiful afternoon,' the man said, hunting for his socks. 'If you wrap up warm, you'll be fine. We can watch the sunset.'

But the woman saw no point in wrapping up warm. Her heart, like her feet, had already gone cold. She did not wish to take in nature's lilac hues, nor immortalise this weekend retreat with intimate, romantic photographs. She wanted to leave then and there. How was she ever going to talk her way out of this? She rifled through the possible excuses. She could say she had an upset stomach. Or a headache. She could say, 'Fine, but I have to wash. Fine but I have sinusitis, there's no way I can go outside with wet hair.'

As he pulled up his zipper, the man began to wonder why she'd suddenly become so coy and demurring. In the nicest way possible, he sat down on the side of the bed and asked, 'Is something wrong? Has something upset you? Didn't you like it?'

The woman tried to quell the guilt rising up inside her. *Dear girl*, she told herself, *this man didn't choose the feet he was born with*. 'No, I'm fine.'

The man stroked the woman's hair. He watched, as the light caught it, and it glinted between his fingers. 'You're so beautiful.'

Accustomed as she was to compliments, the woman attempted to deflect this with another impish smile, and scurried away to gather up her clothes. On entering the room, they'd fallen upon one another so hungrily you'd have thought they were dying of starvation, and now the floor was covered with jumpers they'd peeled off and shirts they'd ripped open, and garments with hooks and eyes that just wouldn't undo. How little time had passed since they bathed in hot springs, gazed into each other's eyes, kissed without pausing for breath, tilted inside the giddy delusion of eternity. But now the man had dressed as fast as he had undressed earlier. 'I'll wait for you downstairs,' he said. 'If you get cold, we can come right back.' Before the woman could think up a new complaint, he added, 'We can get the binoculars from the car, and the water canteen, too – you might get thirsty.' With that, he raced out of the room, as if to stop the world from turning.

Once in the shower, the woman just stood there, arms dangling as she let the spray hit her face, waiting for some part of her hardened heart to melt. If she no longer liked this man, she would have to break it off. In the past, when relationships ended just after making love for the first time, she'd tended to be the victim. More than once she'd paid the price for the satisfaction that came with unravelling the puzzle, after days of catching the scent of a man's skin, and wondering. Some got upset stomachs before they sated themselves, just from arousal. But for her it was different. The only thing that upset her was a pair of ugly feet. And even if she couldn't name that thing – the quality that made some men's feet unlovable – she knew it eventually rose up through their bodies, like mercury.

But how good he had looked to her at first sight. The little ringlets falling over his forehead, the creases in that forehead that gave him such gravitas, the shapely sideburns, accentuating his dimples, the way his teeth sparkled when he smiled, the way he towered over the rest of them and then bent over in humility, the athletic body that he hid inside that camel hair jacket that suited him so well; his confident hands, the way he could hold a glass or a lighter by the tips of his fingers without ever dropping it… So handsome, in fact, that she'd followed him to the back of the gallery to examine him more closely. Even now, she thrilled to the enchantment of that first encounter, as the last flakes fell from the dead skin of her love. She would scrape herself clean. She would have an early night, and use the edge of the pillow to keep herself and this man from touching, and in the morning, after breakfast, she would insist that they leave. When he asked her why, she would make him feel her misery. A cruel caprice. She knew how to handle those who doted on her.

The sky was almost cloudless. The year's growth – the still-fresh leaves, the wild, knee-high grass – wrapped themselves around the trees like a long green girdle. As they climbed up the path leading through the wild brambles and up into the mountains, the woman lagged behind to pick wild flowers she didn't know the names of, so as not to hold that man's hand. To hide her bruises, which were beginning to show now, she wrapped her pomegranate-coloured shawl around her neck. Struggling to keep her balance in her unsuitable shoes, she picked her way across the rough terrain. The man, meanwhile, looked accustomed to mountain treks. Gripping his water canteen, his binoculars swinging from his neck, he strode forcefully uphill like a commando heading for the summit. The woman stopped, and for a while she watched him from behind. With each step, he crushed tendrils that had strayed from the root. With each crunching stride, he violated the silence of the copse, flattening the undergrowth as he pressed on.

He'd forgotten the woman was even there: all that remained of her now were enchanted images of their lovemaking; she'd ceased even to be the subject of those images. The dream that pulsed through him was gentler and lovelier; it grew his own hair a little longer, enlarged his eyes, fattened his lips, exalted his manhood. He'd mastered the grand design that love brought to a man's eyes. He'd stretched it to its limit. He had, in so doing, conjured up a woman whose beauty knew no equal. He looked ahead to the bright paths opening up through the pine trees, and paused for a moment to catch his breath. His lover had fallen well behind, and she was staring up at him, shaking uncontrollably.

In a stentorian voice he called out, 'You're not tired yet, are you?' Saying nothing, the woman continued towards him, this man who now began to change before her eyes, to become as square as the checks in his woodsman shirt. How thick his calves were! He was neckless, and lipless, and his fleshy face was speckled with beads of sweat. Now he wrapped his wide arms around her, as if to lock her inside an iron cage. 'We can't have you getting cold,' he said.

Freeing her head from his armpit, she was only just able to say, 'The weather is beautiful. I'm not as cold as I thought.' The bells of a distant herd of sheep reassured her they were not alone. She looked around her. 'Do you think we might see some sheep?'

The man stroked her hair in a fatherly fashion and said, 'We could, most certainly. They take the sheep in at around this time.'

Looking into her eyes, he could see how much she wanted this moment to be immortal. As he gazed at this woman who'd ignited his dreams with a thousand different smiles; who with her every phone call had brought a boundless light to each day, he was overcome by the desire to show her something she would never forget, something so special, so distinct, that he would be different, in her eyes, from all other men – and thus be the only man in the world. He pressed his lips against hers, and there, for a long time, he stayed. He breathed in the trembling of her face in his hands, and the calming fragrance of her shampoo. The moment they parted, he spied a pine comb just behind her, and that was when he knew he had found the thing he would show her, and that she would never forget.

It was just what he'd been looking for: a young pine, less than five years old, not yet as tall as a man, its needles green and raw. He walked around it, inspecting it with awe, pressed his nose against the bark to take in its texture, its smell. Then he took a penknife with a horned handle from his back pocket. Without ceremony, he put the blade of the knife against the bark and began to peel it like an apple. Beneath the bark, there was a thick, fragrant, golden resin, and as it dripped into the canteen cup in his other hand, the air between the tree and the woman, the woman and the tree, began to tremble, began to shriek, for neither could bear him.

The man never once took his eyes off his penknife; licking his lips, he stripped the fresh bark, just as carefully as if he were skinning a human being without wasting a single drop of blood. He must have known his surgery was opening up deep wounds in that sapling, that it would teem with insects, unable to protect itself, wounded beyond healing, a skeleton of knobs and branches. All this he did for the woman – for his jasmine-scented, raven-haired love.

After he'd stripped the sapling of its bark, and placed his cup at its base, the man began to stretch. His shoulders grew higher, his hands larger, his eyes more magnificent. With every deep breath, he grew in stature. As his cup filled with the tree's sap, he gave into his reveries, drinking in the sweet murmurs that chimed in his ears. Face to face with this rooted and defenceless thing, he was slowly, calmly stealing its life-blood, its hidden light.

By now, the night's scarlet curtain had fallen over the setting sun. The pine needles were a silhouette of pain. The man stamped his feet against the chill – those wide platforms, those fat-toed monsters, those horns of desire, cold as stone – and he looked down at the half-filled cup. Just one sip. One tiny sip, to nourish a force that knew no master. It played on his tongue, with the lilt of eternal peace, cleansed him with fire, cascading through him, burning his insides. He turned around to offer the cup to the woman. And there, in mid-air, his hand remained.

## About the Author

**Sema Kaygusuz** published her debut novel, *Yere Düşen Dualar* ('Prayers Falling on Earth') in 2006. Her 2009 novel *Yüzünde Bir Yer* ('A Spot on Your Face'), was inspired by her own grandmother, and deals with the shame and guilt experienced by someone who survives a massacre. In 2006, she co-wrote the screenplay for Yeşim Ustaoğlu's film *Pandora'nin Kutusu* ('Pandora's Box'), which won the Golden Shell at the 2008 International Film Festival in Donostia/San Sebastian. In 2013 she wrote *Sultan ve Şair* (The Sultan and the Poet), her first theatre play. Kaygusuz is a recipient of the Balkanika Award, the Cevdet-Kudret Literature Award and the France-Turquie Literary Award.

## About the Translator

**Maureen Freely** is an author, journalist, translator and academic, who has written several non-fiction books as well as seven novels, including her most recent, *Sailing Through Byzantium*. She is perhaps best known as the translator of five books by the Turkish Nobel Laureate, Orhan Pamuk. A Fellow of the Royal Society of Literature, and formerly chair of the Translators Association, she is currently the President of English PEN.